Kissing the Captain

A Roses of Ridgeway Novella

Kianna Alexander

Copyright © 2012 Kianna Alexander

All rights reserved.

ISBN:1466208376
ISBN-13: 978-1466208377

This book is a work of fiction. Any resemblance to actual places, people, and events is purely coincidental, or used in a fictitious manner.

DEDICATION

In memory of Mrs. Sue Smith Liner, who during 33 years of dedicated service at Orange High School in Hillsborough, NC touched so many lives, mine among them.

Other Works by Kianna Alexander

Single Title
Skye's the Limit
Red Rose Publishing, August 2009
ISBN 978-16048506

Roses of Ridgeway Series
Kissing the Captain, #1

The Preacher's Paramour, #2
Coming Summer 2012

Loving the Lawman, #3
Coming Fall 2012

ACKNOWLEDGMENTS

The support of my readers is a very important thing to me, so I want to sincerely thank you for taking the time to read this book. I'd also like to thank the ladies of AKRWA (Alaska Romance Writers of America), who gave some insightful critiques on the story when it was still in its infancy. I'd also like to thank the members of HCRW (Heart of Carolina Romance Writers) for their enthusiastic cheer-leading and support. And of course, I thank the illustrious Beverly Jenkins, who inspired me to delve into historical romance in the first place. Happy Reading!

-Kianna

CHAPTER ONE

Northwestern California

April, 1879

Draped in black mourning clothes, Lilly Warren sat on the old oak rocker on the front porch. Beside her on an upside down barrel was her untouched tumbler of lemonade. A weariness reserved for those well beyond her twenty-four years of age gripped her soul like a spider holding its prey.

The bounty of spring's first blush lay before her. The green branches of pines and oaks shaded the house from the sun, and the blooms of golden poppies, violas, and verbena filled the landscape with color and life. Yet on the inside, she wilted.

"Lilly, you must eat or drink something. Your pa would want you to."

She turned to face Prudence, who stepped out of the house. The way her best friend's face appeared lined with concern told her much. "I'm not inclined, Pru."

Prudence folded her arms across her chest. "Three days have gone by since we buried your pa. You can't go on this way, without nourishment." Brushing her hands over her plain brown day skirt, she sat at Lilly's feet. "Besides, the lawyer will be here any minute. Do you want him to see you in such distress, and wearing that sour puss?"

Lilly felt a smile play over her face for a brief moment. She sighed. "I know you're trying to cheer me, Pru. I just can't believe Pa is... gone."

Her friend looked wistful. "I shall miss Mr. Warren. He was a good man." Eyes wide and damp with emotion, she continued, "And I know he would want happiness for his only child."

"I only wish we had known his ague was really the influenza." She swept away a tear falling down her cheek.

Ever the optimist, Prudence patted her leg. "Time to acknowledge the corn. You just inherited twenty-six acres of the most fertile California land there is."

"That may be so, but there is only one of me." She let her head fall back against the rocker. She knew little to nothing about the finer points of the farm's operations. "Who will help me plant the fields, care for the animals, bring in the harvest?"

"I will do whatever I can to help, Lilly. And I am sure you can hire a hand or two in town."

The sound of creaking wheels caught their attention. Lilly eyed the approaching carriage. "I suppose that is Pa's lawyer now."

The covered vehicle, drawn by two horses, pulled to a stop in front of the farmhouse. The driver hopped down from the seat and opened the door. A well-dressed Englishman of about forty exited the carriage, leather satchel in hand.

"Miss Warren?" The Englishman stood at the foot of the porch steps.

"Yes. You must be Mr. Peters."

"I am. Pleased to meet you, miss. And may I offer my sympathies on your father's passing." He tipped his black bowler hat.

She nodded. "Thank you, sir. Please, sit." She gestured to the empty rocker on the other side of her barrel table. "This is my friend, Prudence."

Prudence smiled. "Hello, sir."

Tipping his hat again, Mr. Peters took his seat. "I'm here to inform you of the details of your father's will." He opened his satchel, shuffling through leaflets of paper until he came to the one he wanted. "Mr. Warren has stipulated ownership of the Warren land belongs to you... and a third party, jointly."

Eyes wide, Lilly sprang up in her rocker. "Who is this third party?"

"His name is Ricardo Benigno, and he is the captain of a shipping vessel. As I understand it, he is also the son of your father's good friend and business partner, Diego."

Her memories of the elder Benigno were vague at best. She could recall him a few times as a child when her father would come back from a shipping expedition. But she had no recollection of meeting this Ricardo person. "Pa expected me to share the land with a complete stranger?"

Mr. Peters nodded. "That is what his will demands, I'm afraid."

Good Lord. She had no idea what to think. Her pa probably thought this was the best way to ensure her comfort and safety, but knowing that did nothing to relieve her apprehension. He'd raised her to take care of her own needs, and find her own way in this world. How could he expect her to meekly go into an arranged marriage? Her limited experience with men left her feeling very anxious about partnering with a strange fellow, a foreigner no less.

The pounding of hoof beats jarred her back to reality. Prudence stood, pointing out toward the fields.

With a sly look on her face, she announced, "Looks as if someone else is coming to call on you, Lilly."

CHAPTER TWO

A black stallion advanced across Lilly's land at a gallop. As the beast neared the house, the rider pulled back on the reigns. His Spanish commands to the animal echoed in the silence.

Mouth aloft, Lilly stared at the handsome man seated on the majestic beast. Initially, she wondered whether rider or mount was more magnificent. As she took in the man's golden face, holding full lips and a pair of black eyes sparkling with mischief, she knew the answer to that riddle.

Long waves of shiny black hair grazed his well-muscled shoulders, bulging beneath a white, fancy collared shirt. His thick legs were encased in form fitting black riding pants capped with low heeled black leather boots.

"Hola." He slipped from the horse's back with an air of grace and confidence. He ascended the steps and knelt before Prudence. "I am Captain Ricardo Benigno, and I am pleased to make your acquaintance, Señorita."

Prudence giggled like a schoolgirl with a new doll. "Likewise, Captain. But I think it is Lilly you want." She stepped aside.

Lilly's heart pounded in her ears as the gallant Spaniard knelt at her feet. "Ah, yes. You are the daughter of my good friend. Pardon me, Señorita Warren," he murmured in his Spanish inflected speech. "I am at your service." He captured her trembling hand in his, raised it to his mustached lips, and kissed it.

When she found her voice, she stammered, "Nice to meet you, Captain."

"Please, call me Ricardo."

She nodded, but not trusting herself to form an intelligent reply, she kept silent.

"I do not mean to disturb you, but I am here to pay a visit to Senor Warren." He looked around, as if expecting him to appear any moment. "I was hoping I could convince him to train my ship's new carpenter. Is he available?"

Prudence immediately fell to the porch floor, looking at a loss for words..

Lilly's breath caught in her chest like a snared animal in a trap. Apparently he was unaware of her father's death. How could she break such distressing news to a man she had only just met? Were it not for the chair supporting her, she would have swooned.

Mr. Peters stepped up. "I'm Maxwell Peters, Mr. Warren's lawyer. I am sorry to inform you that he passed away about a fortnight ago."

Ricardo's face fell, the handsome smile replaced by a wistful look. "I am sorry for your loss, Señorita. Senor Warren was a fine man, sailor, and craftsman. I only wish I had the occasion of docking in San Francisco sooner, so I might have seen him one last time."

Lilly grabbed her tumbler of lemonade and took a long drink, lest she faint dead away. Suddenly, the rising heat of spring seemed more stifling than ever. She tugged at the collar of her black shirtwaist, wishing she could loosen a button or two. Being in mixed company made that impossible, so she dabbed at her neck with her handkerchief to catch the perspiration forming there. She did not need a shock like this to cope with on top of her father's demise.

While she pondered her increasingly complicated situation, Prudence batted her eyes at him. "What brings you to California, Captain?"

He ran a hand through his dark, lustrous hair. "I was delivering a quantity of perfumes and spices to the markets in San Francisco. I thought I would call on Leonard while I was here. I have not seen him in quite a few years."

Mr. Peters launched into a speech. "Well, in a way, it is fortunate that you decided to visit, because you are named in Mr. Warren's will."

His eyes widened with surprise. "Truly? I always looked up to Senor Warren, and I'm touched that he thought of me." He stroked his chin, as if thinking. "What are the terms of the will?"

Lilly groaned inwardly. Addressing this now, when they had only just met, seemed ill advised. But if the lawyer insisted, what choice did she have?

"It grants you the rights to this twenty-six acre plot," Mr. Peters answered. "With a stipulation that you wed his daughter."

Sure she'd heard wrong, she massage her aching temple.

This couldn't be happening. Her heart raced, and her stomach felt as if it were filled with lead.

The captain looked thoughtful for a moment, then smiled broadly. "Then I will do it."

She gazed into his coal colored eyes, found them twinkling with some unidentifiable gleam. If he found some humor in this situation, she failed to see it. "What?"

"Do not worry, Bella. I will treat you well." Ricardo stood, bowed. "And I will protect you and our property from all who threaten it."

She was so stunned, she thought her eyeballs might pop out of her head. "I don't know who is more crazy, you, for agreeing to marry a woman you just met, or my father, for arranging this travesty in the first place!"

He shrugged. "You are beautiful, and I can sense your sass and fire. I have grown tired of life at sea, so why not?"

Amazed at his nonchalant approach to this lifetime commitment, Lilly drew in a deep breath. She sensed there was a reason he claimed to be tired of sailing, something he would be hard pressed to reveal. At the moment, though, his reasons for accepting her as his wife were less important than what lay ahead for her. Anger and frustration coursed through her so strongly she feared her blood boiled. Wiping her sweat dampened palms on the front of her skirt, she turned a hopeful gaze on Mr. Peters. "Is there any clause that allows me to shirk this union, and still remain on the land?

The solemn faced lawyer shook his head. "I'm afraid not, Ms. Warren. If you don't wed the captain within two months of your father's passing, you'll lose your claim to the land."

A bitter chuckle escaped her throat. "Well, isn't this a fine fix." Her father's meddling from beyond the grave, while well intentioned, had her mad as a March hare. How could he have done such a thing? She could feel the tears stinging the corners of her eyes, but she refused to shed them, lest she look like a pouting child in front of her company. She was a woman full grown, so she'd do what was necessary to preserve the family lands.

Her knowledge about running the farm was limited at best, since she had only assisted her father in a few of the many tasks required. Also, she did need someone to help work the land, and no one else had offered their services. What choice did she have? She looked to Prudence, who seemed somewhat recovered from her shock. "Well, Pru, I suppose we've a wedding to prepare for." Swinging a cool gaze toward the gorgeous, dark haired man who would be her husband, she announced, "This will be a marriage in name only, Captain."

He met the challenge in her eyes easily. "As you wish, Senorita." He captured her hand again, and brought it to his lips. "But be aware, I will court you."

The contact of his warm lips against her trembling hand was brief, but still left her far more affected than she cared to admit. Vowing to ignore the riotous sensations he invoked, she nodded, but said no more.

CHAPTER THREE

As night fell, Ricardo stood in the parlor window of the modest farmhouse and looked out over the land that would soon be his. Twenty-six acres of fertile land, as well as a passel of livestock would soon become his livelihood and responsibility.

The most important responsibility he would gain, though, was a lovely, but reluctant bride. He turned away from the window, his gaze landing on Lilly. She sat at the kitchen's table, reading an edition of Harper's Weekly by lamplight.

Even the rising shadows of twilight did nothing to diminish her beauty. Her honey brown skin and deep tawny eyes called to him, tugging at his very soul like the siren's song. The long, thick locks of her dark hair, bound in a knot low on her head, beckoned to his fingertips. And her shapely hips and ample bosom, beneath the mourning weeds she still wore, were prizes he hoped to soon claim.

When he'd last corresponded with Senor Warren, the elder man had spoken highly of his lovely daughter. Thinking the old man's words were merely the crowing of a proud father, he'd never have imagined she'd posses such dark, exotic beauty. If she ever succumbed to his wooing, the farmer's daughter would be the boon of a lifetime. Part of him wondered if he'd been to quick to accept the terms of the will. But as a man of his word, he could not very well back out now.

As if she sensed his scrutiny, she glanced up and connected with his watching eyes. "Captain, do you require a beverage, or perhaps another serving of food?"

"No, Bella." The hearty stew and fluffy biscuits she'd served him would sustain him well into the next day.

"Then why do you regard me so?"

"I apologize." He crossed the room, his boots sounding against the well-scrubbed wooden floor, until he joined her at the table. "I was merely admiring your beauty."

In the lamplight, he saw a blush of redness fill her cheeks, and she smiled halfheartedly. "Your words are very kind, Captain. While I have been referred to by many terms, 'beautiful' is not among them."

"Are the men in this country blind, or simply of low intelligence?" He occupied the chair next to her. "I can't imagine no one has ever told you how lovely you are."

"Well, my Pa, but he's supposed to say that."

"Regardless of what you have been called, you should know that you are as beautiful as a sunset at sea, Señorita." Unable to stop himself, he reached out, tracing his fingertip along the smooth curve of her jaw.

She shivered, moved away from him.

"Forgive me. I did not mean to make you uncomfortable."

She drew a shaky breath. "So, tell me about yourself, Captain."

He chuckled inwardly. If she needed to change the subject, he'd oblige her. "Let's see. I am thirty years old. I am from Barcelona, and my family is in the business of shipping spices and perfumes, mostly saffron, from Spain to the world at large."

"So, what's the name of your ship?"

"I dubbed my vessel the Anna Juanita, after my dear mother." He paused as a thought entered his mind. "What happened to your mother, if you don't mind my asking?"

She hesitated. "My mother, Maria, was Portuguese. Pa met her on one of his shipping excursions with your father. She fell off a horse when I was still a young child." She gazed out into the growing darkness of the night, as if remembering something. "My father referred to her as 'his little pistol'. She was feisty, outspoken, and had a true zest for life."

Sensing the pain in her voice, he touched her hand. "I'm sorry. I hope I haven't caused you distress." He slid his hand up her arm, found the bundle of hair at her nape. "I would love to see your hair unbound..."

Her hand grasped his, pulled it away from her neck. "That's not proper, Captain."

A wicked smile turned up the corner of his lips. "Now that you mention it, I've some other improper intentions for you, Bella..."

She dropped her eyes back to her reading. "In that case, I'll have to ask you to take a room elsewhere. There's a boardinghouse in town."

He smiled, amused by her trepidation. "I understand your position, Señorita. But in order for me to protect my interests, I must remain on the land. I will simply sleep in the barn."

She nodded. "I thank you for that, Captain."

"Please, call me Ricardo."

"Ricardo."

His name on her lips sounded as sweet as the song of the sea. In a day or two, he'd fetch his belongings from the ship, and enjoy teasing his second mate, Antonio. He couldn't resist boasting about the bronze beauty who would soon grace his arm and his bed. "Good night, Señorita."

She didn't look up. "Good night."

He left the house through the back door. Outside under the moonlight, he gathered a few things from the pack he'd secured to his stallion's saddle, then retired to the barn.

Lying on a heap of hay, Ricardo mused on his good fortune. The shipping of spices and goods from his homeland had been lucrative for him. For years, he'd sold his wares throughout the civilized parts of the world. With the aid of Antonio, his faithful first mate, and his motley crew of Spanish sailors, he'd traveled the endless blue oceans and beheld some of the most breathtaking sights a man could hope to lay eyes on. The sun rising over the vineyards in France and setting over the Coliseum in Greece. The bright colored costumes of islanders welcoming him and his crew ashore.

As of late, the sea had been an especially hard mistress. Ever since the serious bout of the ague had stricken him several months ago, he found himself unable to tolerate being on the Anna Juanita. Even though the ague had eventually lifted, the vertigo that came with it remained. The churning of the sea and the rise and fall of the boat sent him reeling, and despite his best efforts, he could not right himself. Many times his crew had watched him toppling over at the slightest dip or sway of the ship, and they enjoyed many a hearty laugh at his expense. Only his first mate, Antonio, and the ship's cook, Martin, had remained loyal, demanding respect for him despite his malady.

But now, if he could maintain the Warren farm, he would have a chance to do as a man was expected: excel at his work. Farming would likely involve a great deal of grueling labor, but as long as he stood on solid ground, he could handle it. The men in his crew lost respect for him when they saw his weakness, thus he vowed to never reveal it to Lilly. She needed to be secure in the knowledge that her husband would be a good provider.

Marrying and remaining on the farm meant settling down and giving up his beloved sea, but he saw no alternative. Besides, the lure of the lovely bride he would take on sweetened the pot.

Eyes closed, he sank into the hay, visions of Lilly's face filling his mind.

CHAPTER FOUR

The door chime sounded as Lilly entered the Ridgeway Mercantile, her purse in hand. As soon as her foot struck the sawdust floor, every set of eyes in the establishment turned on her. She waved, acknowledging the smiles and greetings of her neighbors. Noting the intense scrutiny, she brushed the journey's trail dust off the bodice of her sapphire traveling costume, which was a fashionable design she and Prudence had sewn. Adjusting the small flowered hat she wore, she made her way past the stack sacks of flour and millet, shelves loaded with candles, soaps, and other goods, and approached the counter.

"Good Morning, Doris. Have you received any new shipments of fabric?"

The clerk nodded, a knowing look in her eyes. "I supposed you'll be wanting white satin?"

Lilly covered her mouth to stifle her gasp, and leaned forward. Dropping her voice to a whisper, she asked, "How do you know?"

The clerk chuckled. "It's all over town. What else is there to do in a place like Ridgeway besides gossip?"

She placed a hand to her forehead. "Well, dash it all." Dealing with the initial shock of her upcoming marriage would have been enough for her. Now she'd have to deal with the whispering and speculation of the whole town.

"Don't worry," the clerk continued. "Most folks are real pleased you're marrying. You'll need the help to keep the farm running."

An awful thought occurred to her. "When you say everybody knows, you don't mean—"

The door chime sounded again, cutting her off.

"Well, well. I hear you're marrying some dirty Spaniard sea dog."

Recognizing the voice, she groaned. Turning toward the door, she was met with the angry eyes and hanging jowls of Ezekiel Martindale. As always, he sported an expensive suit. His big belly leaked from beneath his fancy jacket and checkered vest, spilling over his pants like water over the falls. The bald top of his head, surrounded by a ring of his graying, once brown hair, shone in the sunlight.

Sighing inwardly, she decided to take the path of politeness. "Good morning, Mr. Martindale."

He closed the distance between them. "Why don't you call me Zeke? All my friends do."

His hot, rancid breath soured her stomach something fierce. "I've been raised to be formal with my elders, Mr. Martindale." She tried, with little success, to hide her disdain for the corpulent, rude man.

He scoffed. "When will you come to your senses, gal? Your Pa may have owned that land, but your still just a half breed. You'd be better off accepting my offer than hitching your wagon to some Spanish sailor, further diluting your African blood."

Being reminded of his offers to marry her increased the turning in the pit of her stomach. Martindale had known her since she was a child, but that didn't stop him from pursuing her as soon as she reached the age of seventeen. She would sooner go to the grave a spinster than spend her days with such a disgusting creature. "While I appreciate your concern for me, I must decline your proposal again."

The clerk chuckled, and Ezekiel puffed up his chest. He banged his large fist on the counter. His round face reddened with anger. "You'll regret this, gal."

He spun, and stormed out. The wooden door slammed in his wake, striking the frame with a loud clap.

Lilly shook her head. "He must think I'm a fool. He doesn't care about me. He's only after my Pa's land." Even if he did care for her, it wouldn't matter because she found the man completely repulsive.

"Been snatching up land ever since he came here during Mr. Lincoln's war." The clerk nodded her agreement. "Anyone with good sense knows that. It's about the last passel of land in the area he doesn't own. So, how much fabric do you need?"

She pulled out the folded Godey's Ladies pattern she'd chosen from her purse. "About six yards."

"You'll make a lovely bride. Let me fetch the fabric for you."

Within a few minutes, Lilly left the mercantile with the wrapped bundle of fabric and a few notions. Climbing onto her waiting buggy, she placed the parcel on the seat next to her and took the reins. Urging her horse forward, she drove down the packed dirt road toward her farm.

On the other side of the street, Ezekiel Martindale stood on the plank walk, watching her drive away, his eyes filled with venom.

She made a show of ignoring him, and continued home.

CHAPTER FIVE

The next day, Prudence showed up at the house bright and early to assist Lilly with the sewing of her wedding dress. The two women sat around the kitchen table, cut pieces of fabric and pattern paper strewn on the table's surface.

Lilly touched the tip of a piece of white thread to her lips to wet it, then maneuvered it into the eye of one of her sharps needles. "I never expected that I'd be working on my own wedding dress." She tied off the end of the thread, sighed. "Especially not without Pa."

Her friend, attaching lace to the end of one of the long sleeves, shook her head. "I know, Lilly. But my daddy will be happy to give you away."

"That's not it. I just didn't expect I'd ever get married."

Prudence looked at her as if she'd turned into a horse. "What did you expect to do with yourself, then?"

She shrugged. "I just wanted to run my seamstress shop out of the house, like I planned to do, and have a few farm hands to help me take care of the farm."

"So, no husband, no children, none of that?"

"No. I want a peaceful life."

"Honey, running a farm and a dress shop all by yourself wasn't gone give you no kind of peaceful life." She finished the first sleeve and picked up the eyelet lace to attach to the second. "After watching my mama and daddy all these years, I think there's a special peace found in the arms of someone you truly love."

Lilly botched a stitch. Tugging it out and redoing it, she countered, "I don't love the Captain. For goodness sake, we only met a couple of days ago."

"He's a handsome man, and he seems real nice. I think you ought to count your blessings and try to make this marriage pleasant." Prudence slip-stitched the end of the lace into place. "I'm jealous, myself. No good looking sailors have set their cap after me lately."

In spite of her frazzled nerves, Lilly chuckled. Pru could always be counted on to make her laugh. "Remember that Easter Sunday when we were about eight?"

"Do I ever. That nasty William Jenkins threw your eggs in the pond, so we waited until he was in the privy and tipped it over." Pru's eyes filled with mirth as she recalled that day. "I can still see him, rolling around in the grass, crying like a big ole baby!"

Both women erupted into peals of laughter, until Lilly found herself wiping the tears from her eyes. "Thanks, Pru. I needed that laugh."

"Nobody was laughing when your mama got a hold of you, though. She gave you such a look I thought for sure she'd kill you."

Lilly could easily recall the cutting eyes of her very upset mother. "She gave me such a lecture, I almost wished she had, it would have been less painful."

Thinking of her mother brought back memories of her singing lullabies in Portuguese, of her delicious spicy stews, and her understanding ways. Lilly missed her fiercely, but tried to push the sadness away.

The top of the dress was beginning to come together, with each of them working on a sleeve. Prudence declared, "Once we finish the bodice, we'll attach the skirt, and finish the embroidery on the bodice. I suppose we can finish it within the next few days."

Taking in the garment, Lilly knew that when it was finished, it would be a lovely dress. She only wished her parents could be there to see her wearing it. A fat tear spilled down her cheek, and she used the back of her hand to quickly dash it away.

Prudence lay a gentle hand on her shoulder. "I know you're missing your folks now, but I've got a little surprise for you that I think might make you feel better."

Dabbing at her eyes, she looked up. "What is it, Pru?"

Prudence gestured toward the front window. "Not what, Lilly. Who."

Looking out the window, Lilly could see a buggy driving to the house. The female driver was hard to make out, until she drew closer to her vantage point. The lady wore a fashionable dove gray traveling costume with a matching hat, and guided the two horse team with surety.

The smiling face of her father's older sister was a welcome sight for Lilly. "Aunt Phyllis!"

Both she and Prudence ran out onto the front porch. Phyllis parked her buggy, set the hand brake, and stepped down. "Lilly, baby, how are you?"

She wrapped her aunt in a tight hug. "Oh, Aunt Phyllis, I'm so glad to see you! I thought you were still in New York with those suffering women."

Aunt Phyllis chuckled, patted her pillbox hat. "Suffragettes, dear. We're working to win the vote. I left as soon as I got the wire telling me of Leonard's passing." She stroked her face. "I'm so sorry I didn't make it in time for the service, but I'm here now."

"It's all right, Aunt Phyllis. I know the cross country journey must be a tedious one. How in the world did Prudence know you were coming?"

"I got into town late last evening and set up at the boardinghouse. Prudence was leaving the mercantile, and she agreed to keep my secret so I could surprise you."

Lilly eyed her friend. "You sly fox. I'll tan your hide later. Right now, come on in the house, Aunt Phyllis."

The three women entered the house, and Lilly and Phyllis reclined on the settee while Prudence occupied the matching armchair.

"So," Phyllis began, "Prudence says you have some very big news to share with me." She trained curious eyes on her niece, and waited.

Cutting her eyes at her friend, Lilly nodded. "Well, it turns out Pa's will left me more than this land. It also assigned me a husband."

Phyllis' eyes grew as large as saucers. "Husband! What in Sam Hill...?"

"I'm getting married. Even from the grave, Pa has managed to choose a suitor for me." She shook her head ruefully.

Her aunt's bottom jaw dropped. "Good grief. You're getting married?"

She nodded.

Prudence piped up. "Oh, and Ms. Warren, he's a Spanish sea captain, and right handsome if you ask me."

Phyllis smiled. "So, he went through with it, then. Your Pa told me about this years ago."

Lilly's interest was piqued. "Do tell, Aunt."

"Back in '61, when you were still a girl, I stayed here with your mama to help care for you while your father was out to sea on a shipping voyage. When he returned, he told me he'd met Diego's son, and that he had his eye on him."

She didn't know whether to be angry or touched. Her father had been thinking about her getting married when she was only six! Knowing him, though, it all stemmed from his desire to make sure she would be cared for. She supposed he'd wanted her to have it all: the ability to take care of herself, and a man in her life. "I can't believe Pa was thinking so far ahead."

Phyllis patted her shoulder. "Leonard was a good man. He would have done anything to secure your future, dear. And now that I'm here, I'll be of service in any way I can."

"I'm glad to hear it, because we still have to finish my wedding dress. The ceremony is in two days' time." She gestured to the pieces of the white satin garment on the kitchen table.

"I'll help you get it finished. I know you'll make a lovely bride. Speaking of which, when do I get to meet this captain of yours?"

"He's gone down to the dock to retrieve some belongings from his ship. He said he would return before sunset." Lilly stood, wringing her hands. "I must admit, Aunt Phyllis, the captain is very...overwhelming."

Phyllis exchanged a knowing look with Prudence. "Don't worry, dear, all the things you're fretting over will happen naturally."

Scandalized, she gasped. Surely her aunt didn't mean..."Aunt Phyllis! I can't lie with the captain. I barely know him!"

Her aunt grinned. "I know that. Don't rush yourself, child. But don't shut the door on marital relations. In time, you'll see the benefit of what I'm saying."

Prudence giggled. "I can already see the benefit, and I haven't known the captain any longer than Lilly." Her eyes took on a wicked glimmer. "He's quite a man."

"Behave yourself, young lady." Phyllis removed her jacket and hat, placing them on the settee. "Let's get to work. That dress isn't gonna make itself."

"Aunt Phyllis, will you stay here at the house? I don't want to be alone with the captain."

"Has he treated you badly? Does he frighten you?"

"No, but...I don't know anything about men."

"Trust me, it's better if you get used to being alone with him." Phyllis ambled over to the table and took a seat. "So when we've finished with this, I'm going back to the boardinghouse for the evening."

Lilly wondered what in the world she was supposed to do with the captain. That made her think about the wedding night. Would he expect her to...?

CHAPTER SIX

Ricardo perused in his chamber aboard the Anna Juanita, being sure to gather all his needed possessions into his carpet bag. The ebb of the water rocked the Anna Juanita gently as it sat docked at the pier. His back pressed against the cabin wall near his bed, he breathed deeply. Doing his best to focus on maintaining his balance, he sat down on his feather mattress. Beyond his closed door, he could hear the voices of his crew as they sang a rousing sea chanty.

A sudden pounding on the door startled him, and he dropped the pair of trousers he was holding. "Who's there?"

"It's Antonio. Open up, Captain!"

"It's not locked."

The heavy wooden door swung on its hinges, and in stepped the bald, burly Spaniard. "What are you about, Captain?"

Ricardo smiled. "I am packing my things to take them to my farm."

"It's not yours yet, is it?"

"No, but it will be in two days' time."

Antonio folded his arms across his wide chest. "What will happen then?"

He'd been waiting for a chance to share the news, and this was the first quiet minute they'd had. "I'm marrying the daughter of Senor Warren."

"Is she easy on the eyes?"

"I assure you, she is a great beauty. She bears the blood of Africa and Portugal, and she has waves of dark hair and the most lovely, shapely figure."

The flash of jealousy filled Antonio's eyes. "I see. I suppose you will be leaving us, then."

He'd tried not to think about the fact that he was giving up his exciting life at sea, but now he had to face it. "Yes. I've a responsibility... I'm fulfilling the last wish of a very good man. You will take over the Anna Juanita as captain in my absence."

Antonio looked thoughtful for a moment, then a big grin filled his bearded face. "A frolic...we've got to have a frolic!"

Ricardo held his hands out in front of him, fending off the idea. "Now, Antonio. I don't know if that's such a good plan."

"O'Course it is! You'll be leaving us soon, and we have to celebrate your last days of freedom." He chuckled. "And my impending assumption of command of this vessel!"

The more he thought about it, the more it seemed logical. "All right, then. But I don't want too much commotion."

By the time the words left his lips, Antonio was already gone, and a cacophony of shouting and cheering could be heard reverberating through the ship. Turning to the porthole, he could see the sun journeying west, and remembered his promise to Lilly to return before sunset. Tossing the last of his things into the two bags he'd brought, he grabbed them and burst out onto the ship's deck.

Gathered around the center mast was the entire contingent of his twenty member crew, cheering boisterously. He smiled and nodded, acknowledging them while doing his level best to steady himself. He thanked the heavens that the ship was docked, and the water was somewhat calm. "I must journey back to the farm. Lilly is expecting me," he called out.

"Aw, she's got a yoke about your neck already!" called a voice in the group. Laughter filled the air. Ricardo felt irritation rising in his gut. It was high time he left the vessel, for his crew no longer saw him as their leader.

"Buenos noches, amigos," he called, and he walked down the ramp that led to the pier. Once on land again, he attached the two bags to the saddle of his rented stallion. Without looking back at the rowdy bunch he called a crew, he spurred the horse on, leaving them and their taunts behind.

When he arrived back at the farmhouse, he stabled his horse and went inside via the back door. As soon as he entered, three sets of female eyes landed on him. Two of them belonged to Lilly and Prudence, but the third belonged to an older, regal woman he didn't recognize. He assumed her to be a relative of Lilly's, because they shared the same rounded chin and wide set eyes. "Hello, ladies."

"Captain, this is my Aunt Phyllis. She arrived in town yesterday." Lilly gestured to the unfamiliar woman.

He approached her, kissed her hand. "It is a pleasure to meet you, Señora Warren."

Phyllis looked impressed. "Likewise, Captain. I can already see why my brother took such a liking to you."

He smiled. Did he sense a bit of flirting in her tone? "Thank you."

She rose from the table. "Prudence, would you see me back to the boardinghouse? I think it's time we left these two to get to know each other."

The giggling Prudence nodded, and she and Phyllis excused themselves.

After they'd gone, Lilly addressed him without meeting his gaze. "I fixed supper. There's ham, green beans, and biscuits."

He recalled the heavenly texture and flavor of her biscuits from last night's dinner. She was quite the cook. If only her demeanor were as enjoyable. "I am ready to eat whenever you are."

"I waited for you to return, because it's the proper thing to do."

He shook his head. Her tone was still so distant. He wondered if he'd ever break through the icy exterior of his intended.

She gestured for him to sit, then placed a plate and a tumbler of lemonade in front of him. Once she'd served herself, she joined him at the table.

"You seem quite young to be captain of a vessel," she offered, taking a bite of the succulent meat. "The few I met when I was young were much older. How did you come to be in command of the Anna Juanita?"

He smiled. At least she was attempting to make conversation. "My older brother, Hernando, was originally the captain. The ship ran aground last year, and he was thrown overboard and into the rocky waters below." He could still see his brother, being carried onshore by the crew, bloodied and broken. "He survived, but his injuries prevented him from returning to command. Being my father's only remaining son, I was given dominion over the vessel."

She looked thoughtful. "You say that as if you did not wish to take over."

"I did, but I knew I could never live up to Hernando in my father's eyes." He stopped himself, lest he reveal more. How had she become so adept at getting him to tell her his life's story?

Perhaps the secret lay in her cooking. Again, her food proved flavorful and well-seasoned. As he savored the offerings she'd prepared, he couldn't help stealing glances at her.

"Even so, you did the honorable thing, by taking over in your brother's stead."

He blinked in surprise. Looking across at her, he saw a ghost of a smile cross her face.

After the remark, she lapsed into silence. It seemed as though he'd finally been able to impress her. He thought she appeared a bit more comfortable with him than she had at their last meal, and that pleased him.

She sat across from him, nibbling at her food in a dainty fashion. Even with the serious look she wore, she remained a vision of loveliness. He wanted nothing more than to slip the pins from her bound hair and rake his fingers through its dark richness, to kiss her mouth and draw groans of surrender from her. But with the expression she wore, he wondered if that would ever be possible.

She looked up from her plate, caught him staring. "What is it?"

I'm wondering how I can get you to give me a chance. "Nothing."

Torchlight and the thundering of hooves broke the silence of the rising night.

Lilly dashed to the front window, with Ricardo close behind. "What in all creation..."

Outside, a conglomeration of buggies and men on horses descended upon the farmhouse. He placed a hand to his temple, cursing inwardly. He grasped her shoulders. "Stay inside. I'll take care of this."

CHAPTER SEVEN

With worry in her eyes, Lilly nodded, and Ricardo opened the front door. The chill of the early spring night met him as he stepped out onto the porch. In the torchlight, he could see many familiar faces, the first of which belonged to Antonio.

Ricardo approached his second mate, seated on a buggy. "What are you all doing here?"

Antonio smiled in the flickering light. "I told you we were gonna have a frolic, Captain!" In response to his declaration, torches and voices were raised against the darkened sky.

"This is not a good time. Lilly and I were just finishing dinner."

Without warning, strong hands grabbed him, lifting him onto the buggy seat next to his second mate. "We aren't here to disturb your intended. We'll take our revelry to the barn, eh?"

Before Ricardo could formulate a response, the buggy was in motion. He supposed at this point, the best thing to do would be to humor his friends and let them make a fuss over him. They'd been out to sea for four months on their journey to California, so they were likely in desperate need of some relaxation.

Shortly, they left the vehicles and horses in the field and went into the barn. Once all the lamps were lit, one of the crewmen took a seat on a bale of hay, producing a fiddle from his cowhide bag. His lively tunes soon filled the air with a sense of merriment.

While enjoying the music, Ricardo took notice of several casks of wine being rolled into the barn. Knowing how rowdy his crew could be when they imbibed, he frowned. "Come now, gentlemen."

Antonio slapped him on the back. "Oh, we'll put a brick in your hat yet, Captain!"

Behind the men rolling the barrels of wine came two scantily clad women, their painted faces plastered with smiles. One was fair, with ringlets of bond curls surrounding her youthful face. The other was older, darker, and more exotic, with rich brown hair falling well past her waist. Both wore similar, garish red dresses, their bosoms spilling forth from the low cut bodices.

Antonio thrust a filled glass into his hand, and Ricardo downed it in one swallow. The wine tasted white, crisp and tart.

Feeling more in the spirit of things, he raised his hands to the two women. "Ladies, I'm the man of the hour. I believe it's me you're seeking."

With smiles and mischievous eyes, they approached him.

"I heard you're a captain," the brunette breathed into his ear, wrapping her arms around his neck. "I'd love to take a sea voyage."

"So would I." The blond echoed her sentiment, and the two women curled themselves around his body like smoke rising from a campfire.

"Oh, Señoritas, how lovely that would be. But alas, I am about to be married."

The blond scoffed. "We know. We heard about your farmer's daughter."

"I bet she doesn't know a thing about pleasing a handsome man like you," cooed the brunette. "Let us take care of you."

Somewhere behind him, a second filled glass was handed to him, and he downed the wine quickly. Through his slightly hooded eyes, he enjoyed the sights and smells of the two willing wenches wound about him.

Until he glanced at the barn doorway.

There, framed by the darkness, stood Lilly.

How long had she been standing there? Long enough, because she appeared so distraught.

Her tawny eyes were wet, red rimmed, and filled with such pain Ricardo was rendered speechless. All he could do was watch as she shook her head, backed away, and ran from the barn, sobbing.

In the following moments, when he regained his senses, he extricated himself from the blonde and the brunette. They mewled protests, but he wrenched away from them nonetheless. "I'm sorry, ladies. There is an important matter I must see to."

He took off at a run, leaving the commotion of the barn behind him as he closed the distance to the farmhouse. Even as he streaked across the fields, he wondered when he'd become so sentimental. He supposed a woman as fiery and beautiful as Lilly could render any man defenseless against such feelings.

When he entered, he followed the sound of her sobbing, and found her sitting on the bottom step of the staircase, head in her hands. Seeing her cry threatened to rend his heart in two, so he reached for her, tried to lay his hand on her shoulder.

But she jumped away as if his hand were a hot iron. "Don't touch me," she insisted through her sobs.

"Bella, please. I did not plan this frolic. My crew... "

"Don't bother." She composed herself a bit, raising her head and using the backs of her hands to wipe her tears away. "You don't love me, I know that. We're only marrying because of Pa's will."

How could he tell her that she was the most beautiful creature he'd ever laid eyes on, that he looked forward to making a life with her? "I am growing to care deeply for you, Lilly. I never meant to hurt you."

She stood, dark eyes blazing with anger. "Then how could you slander me so? Cavorting with those cat house queens. How can you expect me to trust you?"

He didn't know what to say, and he knew the guilt was showing on his face. But they weren't yet married. Why was she making this such a crusade?

She sighed heavily. "Make sure your ruffians return my property to its original state before they leave. And until the wedding," she turned and started up the stairs, "I suggest you keep your distance."

He called after her. "Lilly, wait. Lilly..."

She ascended to the second floor, and he heard a door slam.

Part of him hated to see her hurt, but the other part of him felt entitled to a celebration. After months at sea, he'd wanted to unwind. He'd been foolish to let the lure of two willing women distract him from the prize he was about to claim.? It had been a long time since he'd woken with warm, soft body next to him, and his bride to be seemed uninterested in anything carnal.

Now here he stood, feeling the effects of the argument they'd just had. How in the world had things gotten so mixed up?

Having no answers to any of the questions plaguing him, he trudged off toward the barn. He'd send the whores away, but he would continue to enjoy the company of his crew. After all, he was not married yet.

CHAPTER EIGHT

As the sun reached its pinnacle the following afternoon, Lilly sat on the front porch with her aunt, snapping green beans for lunch. Ricardo had yet to show his face, and that was fine by her. She didn't want to see him after the betrayal he'd dealt her.

"What did he do, Lilly?" Phyllis's voice cut into her thoughts.

"I don't want to talk about it, Aunt Phyllis."

"Lilly, I didn't make a cross country journey just to sit on the porch and watch you frown like you are sucking lemons. I came here to see about you, now what's the matter?"

She sighed, dropping two halves of a bean into her bowl. "Ricardo's crew showed up here last night, and they had some kind of sinful gathering in the barn. Supposedly they were celebrating our upcoming marriage, but they didn't invite me."

Phyllis wrinkled her brow. "How do you know their frolic was sinful?"

"I went out there last night to take a look. The whole barn smelled to high heaven with wine, and two cat house women were wrapped around Ricardo."

"Sounds like sour persimmons. How can you be jealous when you barely know the captain, and claim that you have no interest in him?"

She didn't care for the I-told-you-so look her aunt was giving her. "Aunt Phyllis, I'm not jealous...I'm just insulted. He was drinking and cavorting with whores!"

Finishing her pile of beans, the older woman slid her bowl aside. "Lilly, you and I both know what's really going on here. I don't approve of him gallivanting with soiled doves any more than you do, but it's not embarrassment that's bothering you. You are jealous, and you know it."

Lilly dropped her head. Was it really jealousy that caused her to react the way she did to seeing Ricardo with those two women?

"Anyway, don't let it sour your chance of enjoying your husband. He made a mistake, and so will you if you live long enough." She playfully pinched her niece's chin.

A smile crept across her face. "If you say so, Aunt Phyllis."

She gathered the two bowls of beans, and took them into the house.

In the kitchen, she washed the beans in a basin of water she'd brought in from the pump earlier. As she tossed them into the pot of boiling water going on the stove, she heard her aunt calling her name from the front porch.

Wiping her hands on the canvas apron covering her muslin dress, she went back to the front porch. "What is it, Aunt Phyllis?"

Phyllis said nothing, instead she pointed. Following the gesture, Lilly saw Ricardo striding across the field toward the house. "You called me out here for that?"

She turned to go back in, but Phyllis grabbed her arm. "Stop being so damn stubborn and talk to the man. I'll see about lunch."

After calling a greeting to Ricardo, Phyllis went into the house, leaving the two of them alone on the porch.

"So, I suppose you've slept off the effects of your little gathering?" She made no effort to mask her snide tone.

He frowned. "Yes, I have. And I'd appreciate it if you stopped looking at me as if I've done something wrong."

She propped her fists on her hips. "Oh, so what you did last night constitutes proper behavior for a man about to take a wife?"

He gripped his temple. "Lilly, I am not going to discuss this with you right now. I've a splitting headache."

"Could it be from all that wine?"

He held his finger aloft, and formulated a response. But before he could speak, he looked away, his attention captured by something else.

She followed his gaze.

A fancy carriage rolled across the open land.

She immediately recognized the vehicle. "What is that nasty Ezekiel Martindale doing here?"

"Who's Ezekiel Martindale?"

"Only the fattest, rudest, most insufferable man you'll ever meet. People only tolerate him because he owns most of the land in the county."

His face took on a look of disdain. "Is he after this land?"

She nodded. "And after my hand in marriage, I'm afraid. I've been turning him down for years, but he acts as if I'm suffering from some kind of mental ailment, and he's waiting for me to 'come to my senses.' "

The scowl Ricardo wore deepened, and he stepped off the porch. "Well, let's just see what the fat man wants."

She followed him to the grassy area in front of the house as the carriage rolled to a stop. The driver jumped down from the seat and opened the door. Ezekiel Martindale climbed out, and his belly preceded him.

The portly, brown skinned land baron immediately turned a disgusted gaze on Ricardo. "You must be the dirty seafaring Spaniard who is stealing my intended."

Ricardo looked as if flames might shoot from his mouth, but thankfully, words came out instead. "Good Afternoon. I see not all the black men in California have manners like the late Senor Warren."

"How dare you insult my manners?" Martindale wagged a pudgy finger in his face.

"Hmm, let's see," Ricardo took on a mocking tone. "Calling on us without prior notice and proceeding to insult your host...I'd say that qualifies as a lack of manners."

The large man's face grew red. Hastily turning away from Ricardo, he faced Lilly. "Gal, this is your last chance to be smart instead of foolish. Marry me, and toss this salty dog back to sea where he belongs!"

She shook her head. "As I told you before, Mr. Martindale, I don't have any desire to marry you." What made him think she wanted to spend the rest of her days lying next to his mountains of fat?

Ricardo stepped between them, arms folded over his chest. "Sir, I find it very brave and very foolish of you to come onto this land and try to steal it, and my intended, right from under my very nose. So I'm going to ask you to leave."

Martindale huffed and puffed like a steam engine. "What if I don't? You can't do anything to me. You're no one. I own half the land in this county!"

"Lilly, what's going on?" Phyllis stood on the porch. She must have slipped out while they'd been talking.

"We have an unwanted visitor," she answered, gesturing to Martindale.

Martindale opened his mouth, as if he were about to say something.

A loud clicking sound interrupted the heated exchange.

All eyes turned to Ricardo, who had a Colt drawn.

He leveled the gun, pointing it at Martindale.

"As sure as I am a son of Spain, you will be leaving here." Ricardo spoke, in a calm, even tone. "I've pulled back the hammer. If you don't get back in that carriage and get off our land, you'll be leaving here in a pine box."

Eyes wide, Martindale jogged the short distance to his carriage. "Drive!" he called to his man, and the carriage was soon in motion. Martindale leaned out the partially opened door as he sped away. "I'll be back, gal!"

Regardless of his threats, Lilly found herself chuckling.

Still in the grips of his male anger, Ricardo was still scowling. He tucked the Colt away in his waistband. "What's so funny?"

"It's just that," she struggled to get the words out through her laughter, "I've known Mr. Martindale for many years, and I've never, ever seen him move that fast!"

At that, Phyllis joined in the laughter. "I can't believe he could haul those rolls of fat at such a speed myself!"

Finally Ricardo's face softened, and soon they were all wiping away tears of mirth. Looking into his smiling face as his hearty laughter filled her ears, she realized he'd already kept his vow to defend her, and their land. *Handsome and gallant- what a combination.* Admiration at his bravery made her heart swell.

Later that evening, after Phyllis had gone back to her room in town, Lilly sat on the back porch with a tumbler of chilled water. She was admiring the sunset when Ricardo approached.

"Tomorrow is first planting, so I'll need you to get up much earlier than you did today so we can sow the fields." She watched him.

He cut her an annoyed look, then nodded. "Do you think that nasty Martindale fellow is a real danger?" He stood over her, hands in his trouser pockets, awaiting her response.

She thought about it, shrugged. "I don't really know. He's always said the same kind of thing to me, so I don't know if he's serious or not."

"Well, just in case, I'm prepared to protect you, and our land." His dark eyes were serious, and he seemed to still be holding on to some of his irritation from Martindale's visit.

She smelled a plot. It would take more than that to get him back in her good graces. "After what you did today, I believe you. But it doesn't mean you can come into the house to sleep."

He groaned, running a hand over his face. "Infuriating woman. What makes you think I would want to?" His stance changed, as if his whole body tensed.

"I don't know, maybe your lascivious behavior last night?"

"For goodness sake, you just assume I had relations with those women, don't you?"

"That's usually what men do, isn't it?"

"You proclaim to know everything about men, don't you?" He sighed loudly. "If that's your way of thinking, you won't ever have to worry about sharing a bed with me." He ran a hand over his flowing dark locks, his face a mask of frustration.

She downed her remaining lemonade, and stood. "Good. So go back to the barn. Good night, Captain." Whirling on her heel she strode into the house and closed the door in his face.

CHAPTER NINE

Ricardo got up with the rising sun. After taking care of his morning needs at the pump and the outhouse, he returned to the barn. There he donned a blue work shirt and an old pair of trousers. Shaking the hay and bramble out of his brogans, he slid his feet into the boots and wandered out of the barn.

The scent of coffee wafted to his nose, so he entered the house through the kitchen door. He found a still warm pot of the brew on the stove. Next to it lay a batch of Lilly's feather light biscuits. Lilly was nowhere in sight, so he helped himself. Pouring himself a cup of coffee, he added a bit of milk from the icebox, then took a few moments to enjoy it with four of the fluffy biscuits.

His morning hunger pangs allayed, he stood and stretched. Lilly might be stubborn and headstrong, but her biscuits were heavenly, and she made a good strong brew.

When he reached the side of the house where the newly plowed rows were waiting to be sown with various vegetables, he found her already there. She knelt between the first two rows, using a mallet to drive a small, hand painted sign into the ground. She'd apparently been there for a time, because he noticed the dampness near the collar of her yellow shirtwaist. Small beads of perspiration gathered on her jawline and neck. She'd bound her hair into a knot at the crown, but a few wisps of it escaped, falling down to frame her lovely, concentration filled face.

Amazing. Even sweating and streaked with soil, she was still a regal beauty.

Hearing him approach, she looked up. "Good Morning, Captain."

He groaned inwardly. She still insisted on calling him that. "Good Morning, Lilly. What do you need me to do first?"

"Well, you can start by sowing the row next to me with squash and corn." She handed him the small paper envelopes containing the seed, and pointed him in the direction she wanted him to go. "The new moon is waxing, so the time is right. The other side over there will be planted with beans and peas."

As he moved by her, he thought he felt her hand brush against his leg. When he sat down in the soil, she had gone back to sowing her own row.

"Why don't you use a seed drill?" He opened one of the envelopes. "It seems that would make things go much faster."

"Pa always hated the newfangled thing. He said the only way to get the satisfaction out of harvesting is if you plant the seed yourself, by hand."

He nodded his understanding. He could see how a man would revel in the feeling of accomplishment that came from putting in a hard day's work. Now that he was off the reeling, rocking ship, with the solid earth beneath him, he planned to put in his fair share of labor. "You have not told me much about the farm. What do I need to know?'

"The farm is twenty-six acres, about half of it is still wooded." She drilled a hole with her fingertip in the moist soil, pressing a seed into it. "We own a good size passel of livestock, five horses, two cows, six laying hens, a rooster, and four pigs."

He didn't want to spend the entire day planting seeds in the ground, and not getting to know his future wife any better. They might be on the outs now, but they had the rest of their lives ahead of them, and they should make the best of it.

To that end, he asked, "So, how long does this usually take?"

"When Pa and I did it, we had a hired hand to help us, but we got in done in one day, so long as we got an early start."

It was small talk and he knew it, but better to make small talk than to argue with his feisty bride to be. Besides, if he planned to be a good provider for her, he had to assess the situation he was stepping into. "Do you know how to contact the hands that were employed here?"

She shook her head. "I really don't know much about this sort of thing. I helped with the planting, milked the cows, and spread feed for the hens." Placing an empty seed pack to the side, she opened a new one. "That is about the extent of my farming expertise."

He covered a seed, then brushed his dirty hands on his trousers. Pulling at his chin, he wondered if she knew how or where to market the harvest. After what she said, it seemed doubtful. "Did you ever sell any of the crops? Or perhaps fresh butter or milk?"

She looked thoughtful. "We did sell some of the vegetables, but I can not recall ever selling milk or butter."

He clapped his hands together. "We must start. There is always a demand for fresh dairy products, Lilly. We can turn more than enough profit from the sale of milk, cream, butter and such to pay for the hands."

"I supposed we could," she said. Her face betrayed her; she found his ideas impressive. "I want to do whatever I can to keep the farm running and solvent." She paused. "For my pa."

He watched her, his heart touched by her words. It was plain that she missed her father fiercely, but beneath her sorrow reined a palpable determination to preserve everything Leonard had worked for. "How did he handle planting days?"

"He used to make two big stacks of pancakes on planting day." She looked toward the rising sun with a wistful glimmer in her eyes. "And we'd talk about everything, politics, religion, life, while we planted the rows." Her voice trailed off, and she wiped away a tear. "I miss him so."

The sight of her crying again tore at him, so he reached out for her. To his surprise, she sank into his arms, resting her back against his chest, and let the sobs she must have been holding in for days escape her throat. He rested his chin in the nest of her rich dark hair and let her cry. She needed to grieve, and he wanted to be there for her. He could only imagine how he would feel if he lost his own father. Regardless of the fact that Hernando was so obviously Diego's favorite, Ricardo knew he would still suffer a great deal when his father passed on.

He said nothing, because he didn't know the words to comfort her. So he held her until the tears subsided.

She wiped at her eyes with the sleeve of her shirtwaist. As if realizing for the first time that he was holding her, she scrambled away from him. "I'm sorry, Captain."

He shook his head. "There is no need to apologize. It is healthy to grieve, especially when the loss is so great." He slid closer to her, streaking his trousers with soil, but not caring. Capturing her hand in his, he whispered to her. "I only hope that I have offered you some comfort."

She looked away. "Captain... " She paused, as if searching for the correct words. "Thank you. For everything."

"You're welcome." He knew she probably referred to his actions with Martindale. He smiled, trying to lighten the mood. "What must I do to get you to call me Ricardo?"

She appeared thoughtful, then tossed back, "Help me get this plot seeded before sundown, and I will call you whatever you wish."

"So be it." The playful tone she took gave him hope that her anger over the frolic might be subsiding.

He hoped so, because he wanted nothing more than to enjoy his marriage. The idea of spending his days with a disagreeable, sour faced woman did not sit well with him. Part of him longed to return to his life at sea, where he did as he pleased, and a willing woman could be found at every port.

But the unrelenting vertigo, that left him clumsy and ill whenever the vessel hit choppy waters, prevented him from it. He had tried every cure known to man, with no results. At this point, returning to the sea was out of the question, no matter how foul tempered his bride might be.

As much as she tried to present herself as serious, practical, and capable, he sensed something beneath the façade she had erected. He watched her, sowing the seeds into the earth with such care, and knew that deep inside of her lurked a fire that only he could bring to its full, glorious blaze.

And, if she let him, he would do just that.

CHAPTER TEN

Lilly stood in the full length mirror that hung on her bedroom wall and surveyed her reflection. The white satin gown that she and Prudence had been sewing on for days had turned out beautifully, from the long, lace capped sleeves to the embroidery on the bodice. Despite her absolute nervousness about her nuptials, the beauty of the garment could not be denied.

"You look beautiful, Lilly." Phyllis, wearing her best yellow satin gown, appeared behind her. "I knew you'd make a lovely bride."

"Thank you. I just hope I don't regret what I'm doing here."

Prudence entered the room, carrying a wreath of pink blossoms she'd fashioned by hand. "Oh, Lil, stop worrying. With a man that handsome, it can't be a mistake."

She didn't deny Ricardo's handsomeness, or his charm. He'd shown himself to be an honorable, brave, and hardworking man. Though she'd thought she'd never marry, she knew she could do much worse in a mate. Lilly smiled despite the butterflies wrestling in her stomach, and stooped a little so that Prudence could place the wreath around her up-swept hair. "Pru, you're such the naughty girl."

Prudence winked, stepped back to admire her work. "It's perfect. You are going to steal the captain's breath."

"Perhaps not, after he spent an evening with those harlots." She looked down at her hands, sheltered within the gloves she'd fashioned of snow white lace. Chastising herself inwardly for still being jealous over the incident, she wished she could snatch the words out of the air and return them to her throat unsaid. Unfortunately there was no going back.

Phyllis interjected. "Now, Lilly, we talked about this. He's a man, just like any other. He may have exercised bad judgment, but after meeting him, I believe he will treat you well. So don't let this harden your heart."

She sighed. She didn't want to forgive Ricardo, but she knew that when it came to men, her aunt's knowledge far outweighed her limited experience. Still, she didn't enjoy the thought that she might have to follow the advice.

"Come on, Lilly. We've got to get you downstairs. Everyone is starting to gather in the back yard." Phyllis took her by the hand and led her out of the room. Prudence followed them, carrying the end of her dress to keep it off the floor.

As they meandered across the kitchen toward the back door, Prudence went out ahead of them. She took her place underneath the borrowed wooden arch, standing next to Sheriff Paul Rogers, and a smiling Ricardo, wearing his pressed uniform and a black Stetson. Even in her state of anxiety, she had to admit he was easy on the eyes.

About fifty guests were present, seated in chairs arranged in rows to form an aisle for her to walk down.

There were members of the crew of the Anna Juanita, townsfolk, and family friends. Sitting near the rear was one of the loose women who'd been in the barn frolic. The blond woman was weeping into a handkerchief, as if distraught. Thinking the woman might be upset about Ricardo's impending marriage gave Lilly a sense of self-satisfaction she would not have expected.

Standing in the door frame grasping her aunt's hand, Lilly looked into the face of the man she was about to marry. His eyes held something deep that she couldn't identify, but it drew her. Just then, a man began to play a lilting melody on the violin. So, she placed a slipper covered foot on the back porch to begin her journey toward the man who would be her future.

***

Ricardo stared at Lilly as she slowly made her way toward him on her aunt's arm. The guests and surroundings faded into obscurity as his focus landed solely on her. She presented the picture of radiance. The white satin gown she wore had obviously been fashioned with care, and gave her a glow of purity and loveliness. He had never in his life laid eyes on a more beautiful sight. Phyllis placed Lilly's hand in his and backed away, and he was left enraptured by her dark eyes.

Sheriff Rogers performed the ceremony, and as Ricardo spoke the words to his bride, Ricardo was startled to realize just how seriously he took his vows. What had started out as escaping the turmoil he felt at sea had become something much more intimidating. Could the feisty farmer's daughter have lain claim to his heart, when he had left a string of mistresses at every stop on his shipping route? The thought bordered on frightening, so he pushed it aside.

Her velvet, feminine voice promised him forever, and he was afraid he wanted it. Not just because of his claim to the fertile tract of land, but because of the woman standing before him. Some nameless quality of this innocent, headstrong woman tugged at his very soul.

With the vows taken, the sheriff pronounced them man and wife. He let his gaze meet hers, and she looked away as if afraid. Capturing her satin jaw in his hands, he lifted her face and touched his lips to hers. Her mouth tasted more wonderful than the finest aged amontillado, and the way she surrendered to the kiss made him want to plunder her sweetness. Grappling with the limits of his self-control, he kept it chaste for the benefit of the crowd. But he couldn't wait to sample the sensuality he sensed lying dormant in his new wife.

When the seal of their lips broke, she scampered away, mumbling about greeting the guests. He watched her retreat with a smile, knowing full well that wasn't what caused her to flee. His virgin bride had tasted passion's opening notes, and taken flight like a startled rabbit.

As the new Mrs. Benigno retreated, he let his eyes sweep the small crowd of attendees. The sight of the blond whore who'd been present at the frolic gave him pause. Her wet, puffy eyes met his, and he frowned. Next to the distraught looking female stood Antonio, who cringed under Ricardo's pointed scrutiny.

Fury burned inside him like chaff set ablaze as he strode across the yard to where his second mate stood. After offering a short, polite nod to the weeping young woman, he dragged Antonio aside by the arm. "What were you thinking, bringing her here?"

Antonio shrugged. "She insisted. She's been on board the ship with us, and I saw no harm in it."

"There is a great deal of harm in it. You've now insulted Lilly twice by bringing loose women onto her land." He held back his anger, lest he challenge his good friend to a duel in front of everyone present. "Get her out of her, Antonio."

With a crooked, sheepish grin, Antonio nodded. "Sorry I've upset your Senora, Ricardo."

As Antonio led the woman away, her blue eyes met his briefly. Her gaze held a female longing he'd seen many times before, but he ignored it. Once he was sure they'd left the gathering, he went in search of Lilly. Even as his anger at Antonio began to subside, he felt guilty for not turning the whores away from the very beginning. The gesture would have spoken volumes to his crew, and possibly prevented Antonio's lapse in judgment today.

The guests mingled and socialized, partaking of the cake and punch the sheriff's wife had prepared for the festivities. Ricardo found Lilly in a small group of women standing on the back porch.

"Excuse me, ladies, but I'd like to borrow my wife for a moment."

Peals of feminine laughter came from the group. "Go ahead, Captain," one of the women said, gently thrusting Lilly toward him.

Tipping his hat in thanks, he grasped her upper arm and guided her away. They came to a stop beneath the shade of a pine tree near the side of the farmhouse.

"What is it, Captain?"

"For goodness sake, Lilly. We are man and wife, and you promised. Call me Ricardo."

She gazed down at the ground, as if concentrating on the grass. "Fine. What can I do for you, Ricardo?"

He wasn't sure he liked the tone she took with him. Was she really annoyed that he took her away from her gossiping girlfriends? It was their wedding day, after all. "What's the matter with you, Bella?"

She turned her back to him. "Oh, I just couldn't guess. Could it be the fact that you brought those whores onto my property?"

Alright, he definitely did not like her tone. "I did not bring or invite them here, my crewmen did, and I know you're acting this way because you assume I had relations with them."

She spun, gave him a cutting look. "You're a man, aren't you?"

For the life of him, he could not guess why she still held onto such jealousy over the incident. Had he not made it clear that those women had not lain with him? "I am, but I also know how to exercise self control." He could feel the heat of anger rising in his chest. "I think it's best we change the subject. I don't want to spend this day fighting with you."

She folded her arms, glaring at him, but said nothing. Even in the beautifully handmade gown, she resembled a little girl pouting over some denied toy.

He found her manner infuriating. "Is it an apology you're after? Because I have done nothing wrong by letting my crewmen throw a frolic in my honor."

She huffed loudly. "Fine, since you feel that way, then you can spend another night in the barn."

Gathering up the voluminous skirt of her white dress, she stomped away. He closed his eyes, leaned back against the sturdiness of the trees' trunk. When he opened them, he could see the curious gazes of some of the wedding guests fixed on him.

Ignoring their stares, he straightened his Stetson and made his way to the trestle table, where the sheriff stood. "Sheriff, thank you for your services today. Could you please see the guests safely off the property?"

Sheriff Rogers nodded, taking the arm of his concerned looking wife. "Sure, captain, if that's what you want."

That done, Ricardo strode through the field toward the house. Whether she liked it or not, Lilly was his wife now, and if she thought he'd be put off by her pouting, she would soon discover just how wrong she was.

CHAPTER ELEVEN

Lilly reclined on her bed, trying to read the latest issue of the Ridgeway Tribune. The town's paper was only two pages, but so few settlements even had a paper at all. As daylight waned, the reading became difficult, so she folded paper and tucked it into her night table drawer. She glanced at her wedding dress, slung over the back of the chair at her sewing table, and groaned. Some wedding night this was turning out to be. Even though she hadn't really expected or wanted to get married, she certainly couldn't have predicted spending the first night of a marriage stewing in her room, while her husband was exiled to the barn. What had she gotten herself into?

He'd proven himself a hard worker by helping her sow the crops, attending to the tedious task with diligence, and without complaint. He'd listened to her memories of her parents, encouraged her, and not called her weak for shedding tears. She'd found a special brand of comfort from her grief in the protective circle of his arms. In all their dealings, he'd been respectful, and had even come to her defense against the foul tempered Martindale. Beyond all those virtues, he possessed such heart-stopping handsomeness, just being near him rendered her somewhat witless.

But she could not simply dismiss the presence of harlots on her land. Even if the crew had been responsible for bringing them, Ricardo should have dismissed them right away. Allowing them to remain at the frolic, and today at the ceremony, spoke of such disregard for her sensibilities, she didn't know how to get past it.

A blast of air blew in through the open window. Pulling her silk wrapper closed over her nightgown to fend off the chill, she lit the gas lamp she kept on her night table, then shuttered the window. Securing the latch, she turned to make her way back to the bed.

And found Ricardo standing in her door way, staring at her.

She tied the belt of her wrapper and crossed her arms over her chest. "What is it now, Ricardo?"

"It is time to turn in for the night, dear wife," he announced, his voice just above a whisper. Then he made the bold move of stepping over the threshold into the room.

Infuriated, she struggled to keep her voice low and respectful. Why, she didn't know. After the blatant disrespect he had shown her, she owed him nothing. "I'm aware of that, but I asked you to sleep in the barn."

"I decided against that. What kind of wedding night would this be if we were separated?" He stepped out of the shadows, entering the ring of light cast by the flickering lamp. "I know you feel betrayed by my behavior, and I apologize. And whether you choose to believe me or not, I did not utilize the services of those women."

She stared at him, standing there in his trousers and shirt. Did she detect sincerity, or was it his charm, matched against her inexperience, that caused such powerful sensations within her? She needed to sit down, and thought it unwise to sit on the bed. So she passed him and took a seat on the chair she kept by her sewing table. "Ricardo, I do not want to talk about this."

He touched her shoulder, and the contact caused a shiver to travel down her spine. "Lilly, I need you to know that I am sincere. When I learned of your father's will, I wanted to do what was right. But when I lay eyes on you..." he turned away briefly, as if searching for the right words. "I now realize what a gift I had been given."

"No amount of your sweet words will erase the memory of you with those loose women, Ricardo." A tear slid down her cheek unbidden, much to her frustration. Why should she even care what lewd behavior he participated in? After all, her mind told her, she did not love him. But her heart hesitated to agree with logic.

"I understand that. I came here to show you my intentions are honorable."

Her eyes wide, she asked, "How do you plan to do that?"

"By inches, if I must. I will only go as far as you let me, but I want to make love to you."

She shuddered. This was the conversation she'd been dreading. Embarrassment reddened her cheeks when she realized what was coming. "Ricardo, I don't know if I'm ready for this." Truly, that was an understatement, she'd never been so conflicted in all her life. Her body had sang at the kiss he'd given her beneath the wedding arch, but she knew nothing about the marriage bed. She had shielded her purity, as her father insisted, but now she as she looked at her new husband she felt as though she lacked something.

He raised a gentle hand, stroked her cheek. "I assume you are a virgin, Bella."

She nodded, her gaze on the floor.

"Do not be ashamed of your virtue, Lilly. I certainly am not." He knelt before the chair, bringing his face level with hers. "If you are willing to learn, my darling, I will teach you love."

What that entailed, she had no idea. Her father's talks about the birds and the bees had been limited at best.

He'd told her that she didn't need to concern herself, because one day her husband would teach her all she needed to know. Now that she was confronted with this overwhelming reality, she didn't know if she was ready to discover all that marital relations could mean. If she could get this worked up over Ricardo with only the limited physical contact they'd shared, what lay ahead for her once his "lessons" began in earnest?

Her breath stacked up in her throat. Another tear slid down her cheek, but this one was motivated by an emotion she couldn't identify. Dashing it away, she drew a labored breath, taking in his masculine scent.

A heartbeat later, he covered her lips with his own. The initial contact lit a fire deep inside her, and she couldn't muster anything resembling resistance.

Her anger and irritation melted away beneath the fiery impetus of his kiss, and soon her tongue, of its own accord, ventured into his mouth.

A guttural groan escaped his throat, and he pulled away. "Before we go any further, you must be sure that you are ready to go down this path. Passion can quickly lead to the point of no return, my darling."

Inside, she melted, swooned, reeled from the first notes of desire singing in her blood. Where this journey would take her, she had no idea, but if the pleasure that radiated through her untutored body was any indication, she did not want it to end.

Touching her kiss swollen lips, she nodded. "I am ready, Ricardo." The whispered words slipped from her lips, and she knew that when morning came, she would be a different woman.

He stood, took her trembling hand in his, and led her to the bed.

CHAPTER TWELVE

Ricardo's eyes slid open, and closed again against the assault of the morning sun streaming through the bedroom window. The open shutters allowed the light, as well as the fresh morning breeze and the lilting notes of the birds' songs, to enter the room.

Allowing his eyes to adjust for a moment, he sighed with contentment. Lilly's warm, soft body was pressed against his. Her soft, breathy snores ruffled the silence.

He did not want to move for fear of waking her. She was so lovely, with the rich darkness of her unbound hair strewn over the pillow. Beneath the coverlets, her bare chest rose and fell in time with her breathing. He could still see the image of her lush nakedness in his minds' eye, but fought the urge to raise the quilts to gaze upon it again.

Placing a gentle kiss on her cheek, he smiled. Their wedding night had been one of the hardest won treasures of his life. She may have been resistant, but when she'd finally surrendered, she'd done so fully and passionately. He would never forget the sight of her taking her pleasure, the feel of her wrapped around him, and the sound of her calling his name. Even now, as he inhaled the lingering fragrance of her sweet perfume, he knew their souls were now bonded together.

She stirred, turning over to face him with sleepy eyes. A smile lit her tawny eyes. "Good Morning."

"Good Morning, my darling." He stroked her cheek with a gentle hand, and she turned her face up toward his kiss. Brushing his lips against hers, he groaned. "We must begin our day soon."

The pools of her tawny eyes reflected her confusion. "Why?"

The innocent question only fueled his desire. "Because if we remain in bed, I will take you again."

She blushed, nodded. She slipped out of bed, giving him a brief glimpse of her nude body before donning her silk wrapper. "I'm going down to the pump."

She left to attend to her needs. While she was gone, he rose and dressed.

When she returned, he was in the kitchen, looking through the cabinets. "Do we have any more coffee?"

She nodded, and fetched a bag of grounds from the pantry. "I'll make some. What would you like for breakfast?"

He sat at the table, stretching his hands behind his head. A man could get used to this kind of treatment. "Whatever you'd like to prepare will be fine with me."

While he waited, she prepared a breakfast of bacon, scrambled eggs, and fried potatoes. His stomach growled as the heavenly aromas of her cooking filled the house. Soon, she sat a filled plate before him, along with a cup of coffee. Taking a bite of the fat yellow eggs, he groaned with delight.

"That good, or that bad?" she asked over her coffee cup.

"It is wonderful. I can honestly say your cooking rivals that of my dear mother."

She blushed again. "Thank you, Ricardo."

"In my mind, this union is off to a very good start." He forked some of the well-seasoned potatoes.

"Well, I want to start working, as soon as is acceptable." She braced herself for his reaction.

He swallowed, surprised. "Working? Working at what?"

"Sewing. I am trained as a seamstress." She sipped her coffee. "I want to run a shop out of the house, but I haven't sewn anything recently except for my wedding dress."

He frowned. This was not part of his idea of a perfect marriage. "Are you sure you wish to work? You will have your hands full taking care of me, and soon, our children."

The sweet calm that had been on her face was quickly replaced with a sour look. "Children?"

"Yes, I assume we will have at least four."

She stood, crossed her arms over her chest. "Excuse me, but I'm the one who will have to carry and deliver these children. I cannot say for sure I want that many. And how soon are you expecting me to bear children?"

"Right away, of course." He pushed his empty plate away. "That is an essential part of marriage."

"So, you expect me to bear your children, stop doing the work I love, and spend my every waking hour caring for a family?"

"Yes." He could not comprehend the contrary tone and sour expression she'd taken on. Was her memory so short that she already forgot the night of ecstasy they'd shared? And what woman didn't want the joys of a husband and family? "What is wrong with that? My dear sainted mother has given her heart and soul to our family for years, and she has found much fulfillment in having a happy family and a peaceful, well maintained household."

She turned away from him. "Well, bully for her, but I require more than that in order to be fulfilled." She cleared the plates, setting them on the counter.

He sighed. Here he was, offering to her the life most women pursued and craved, and she was throwing it back in his face. It seemed his new bride held some very unconventional beliefs about her role in a marriage. "All right, I will compromise with you. If you can find time enough to sew, in addition to helping me with the tasks of running this farm, I will allow it."

She faced him again, her eyes flashing with anger. "Allow me? Are you mad? I have trained since I was a girl to take up dressmaking. Now, I intend to do it and I don't need your permission." She started to walk away, then turned back. "And another thing. I am perfectly capable of managing money, and I will not be turning my profits over to you. Contrary to what you and my late father may believe, I can take care of myself." That said, she stormed out. Seconds later, he heard her stomping up the stairs.

Rubbing a hand over his weary eyes, he rose from his seat. "What in the world is the matter with her?" After everything they'd shared, he couldn't imagine why she was acting this way. What woman wouldn't want to settle down with him, bear his children, and not have to worry about anything outside her own household?

He needed to know what she found so unappealing about his expectations, so he went upstairs. Approaching the bedroom door, he turned the knob only to find it locked. "Lilly? Let me in."

"I am not dressed yet," she called.

He couldn't stifle his chuckle. "That's fine, my darling. I have already beheld all your naked beauty."

A heavy thud on the other side of the wood caused him to jump away from the door.

"That was one of my brogans," she called. "If you don't wish to be struck in the head with one, you should step away from the door until I'm dressed!"

Groaning, he slid down the wall and sat on the floor.

***

Lilly pulled on her skirt and slid her feet into a pair of soft soled slippers. She couldn't believe Ricardo's single minded male pigheadedness.

Truly, what they'd shared the previous night had branded her heart. She could never have imagined that surrendering her virginity to her new husband could be so life altering. Even now, as she gazed at the spot on the sheets that proved what she'd given him, her body echoed with the erotic memories of his touch, his kiss.

She'd been sewing since her twelfth year, and it had taken her all those years to build up her skill.

How could he expect her to give up everything she'd worked so hard to build?

Her father had been so adamant that she learn a trade, so that she would be able to earn a living. If she ended up in dire straits, he'd said, she'd have a skill that would keep her from becoming destitute. Now that this marriage had begun, the independent, competent side of herself was at war with the side that suddenly craved all the attention, care, and affection her new husband offered. In the last month, her world had changed so much. Her confusion over what she wanted simply piled on the agony.

Once she was dressed, she opened the door and found him sitting on the floor in the hall. He appeared very pitiful, sitting there like a child scolded by his mother. On his face was a look that combined confusion and exasperation.

"Will you speak to me now, or are you going to strike me with your boot?" He looked up from his seat, waiting for her response.

"Yes, long enough to tell you that I am not going to let you dictate my life, Ricardo." As handsome as he looked in his tight fitting black trousers and white ruffle collared shirt, and as amazing as his lovemaking had been, she would not be led through life like some mindless puppet.

"I am not attempting to dictate your life. I merely thought you would enjoy living a comfortable life, with no work required on your part outside of caring for your family." He rested his head in his hands. "Isn't that what all senoritas desire ?"

She propped her fists on her hips. "Possibly, but I am not your average senorita." As much as she enjoyed looking down on his arrogant self, she plopped down on the floor next to him. "If we are going to be together, we need to discuss these kinds of things."

He gazed at her, and she saw the determination in his black eyes. When he spoke, he did so with conviction. "In my world, raising families and running households are the only tasks a woman is expected to do. I have watched my mother, grandmother, and several aunts do it. All my life, that is all I have been exposed to. Why is this not enough for you?"

She shook her head. "I understand most women can be happy in pouring themselves into family. But I need more. Did you know that I have been sewing for twelve years, and that my work has allowed me to put away a sum of money to care for myself?"

Eyes wide with shock, his mouth hung open for a moment. "No. I did not know this. Did your father know about it?"

She nodded. "He was the one who encouraged me to be independent, to support myself. It is one of the most important values he ever taught me."

"I don't know how I feel about all this, Lilly." He looked away, ran a hand through his dark, wavy locks.

"I am trying to compromise with you, Ricardo. I will even consider bearing babies for you. But I won't give up my sewing."

"I want to be your provider and protector. If you can do all these things for yourself, then why would you need me around?"

What kind of idiotic question was that? Irritated, she stood. "I guess I don't."

And without waiting for his response, she stalked off, intent on completing the days' housework, and avoiding her husband and his bruised ego.

CHAPTER THIRTEEN

As the sun dipped low on the horizon, Lilly hauled the water from the pump she would need to take a bath. The last of the water in the house had gone to wash the dishes from their simple supper of roast chicken, corn, and bread.

Ricardo, sitting at the kitchen table, pored over a small stack of papers. He called to her as she entered with the first bucket. "Why don't you let me help you with that?"

"You look like you're busy," she answered, pouring the water into the cauldron atop the stove. "What is that you're looking at, anyway?"

"It's an inventory from my last shipping voyage. But I can put it aside long enough to haul that water for you."

She hated to admit it, but she relished the idea of him hauling the heavy bucket back and forth, especially since she was exhausted from the days' work, and at least three more trips to the pump would be necessary to gather enough water for a decent bath. Blowing out a breath, she acquiesced. "All right. I am hanging up my fiddle. You take over, Captain."

"Excuse me, but we had an agreement." He stood, his eyes twinkling with mischief.

She couldn't help thinking that made him all the more handsome. "I'm sorry. I meant to say, you can take over, Ricardo." She emphasized his given name.

He smiled, showing his rows of beautiful teeth. "Thank you, Señora. That is much better. Now, how many buckets will you be needing?"

"Well, I am desperately in need of a hot bath, so I'll need three more."

A look came over his face, and she wondered if he were imagining her in the bath. "In that case, I will bring four."

Before she could address him, he disappeared out the back door. Thinking it best to distance herself from her charming captain for the time being, she made her way upstairs to prepare for her bath.

The first task consisted of dragging the large, claw footed bathing tub out of the corner of the extra bedroom where it was kept. With that done, she opened the wooden shudders to let in the fresh evening breeze. She knew from experience that once the steamy water heated the small room up, she would appreciate the fresh air.

Going down the hall, she entered her own bedroom and gathered her nightgown, wrapper, a small cloth, bar of soap, and a bathing sheet. With the bundle of items in her hand, she returned to the extra room where the tub sat, ready to be filled. On the way, she stopped before her father's closed bedroom door.

She had avoided entering the room since her father's death, but now something drew her inside. Setting her things by the door, she turned the knob and stepped into the darkened space.

The pipe tobacco her father had favored scented the air with a tart sweetness. His pipe and his favorite hat lay atop the rumpled bed sheets, and his old oak cane leaned against the foot of his pine bed frame. Everything in the room remained just as he left it.

She could not bring herself to make the bed, because she could not bear to disturb anything. She needed the room to remain the way it was, as a sort of memorial to the man he had been. How long his things would have to stay this way remained to be seen, but as she looked at the possessions of the only man she had ever truly trusted and loved, moving them seemed somehow wrong. With a heavy heart, she slipped from the room, and closed the door behind her.

She took her things and waited by the big tub, until she heard Ricardo's footfalls ascending the stairs. "I'm in here," she called, to guide him to the right room.

He soon appeared in the door frame, and to her surprise, he was shirtless. The sheen of perspiration glistening on his bare chest betrayed his labor at hauling her water, and she watched with great interest as he poured the large cauldron of steaming hot liquid into the tub.

"There you are," he announced, sitting the empty cauldron down. "I have something for you."

Curious, she asked, "What is it?"

He reached into the pocket of his dirt streaked trousers, and pulled out a small paper wrapped object. "It's scented soap. I picked it up on the sea voyage to California."

Taking the bar from his hand, she raised it to her nose and inhaled its scent. It smelled fresh, exotic, like orchids and roses. "This is the sort of cargo you handled?"

He nodded. "I had some left over from this last trip. I thought you might like it."

No man had ever given her a gift before, and she knew she would enjoy the sweet smelling soap better than her plain bar. "Thank you, Ricardo."

"You are most welcome, Lilly." Lifting the empty cauldron, he turned from her. "I'll wait downstairs while you take your bath."

As he walked away, she found it hard to tear her gaze from his well-muscled back and his round bottom. Scandalized by her own thoughts, she began to undress. But even the welcome embrace of the hot water surrounding her did little to chase away her fantasies of Ricardo. She envisioned herself, wrapped in his protective embrace, being swept away by his kiss...

Visions of the passion they had shared danced in her mind. His rugged, gruff exterior belied the gentle, fiery tutelage he had treated her to. She could still hear his whispered promises of forever, and his declarations of his intent to gift her with all the pleasure a woman could hold.

She reclined there, fantasizing so hard and so long the water began to cool around her. Feeling the chill, she unwrapped the soap and cleansed her body quickly, but thoroughly. Then she emerged from the tub, feeling refreshed and renewed.

Donning her nightgown and wrapper, she slipped her feet into a pair of comfortable slippers and glided toward the stairs.

She found Ricardo, sitting by the front window. He'd lit a lantern and placed it on the windowsill. The small circle of light the lantern provided illuminated his handsome face in the dim shadows of the room. Across his lap lay the stack of papers she had seen him looking at earlier. Propped next to him, against the wall, stood a Winchester repeating rifle. She supposed that's what he referred to when he vowed his protection over her and the property.

He looked up from his papers, smiled that gorgeous smile. Inhaling deeply, he commented, "You smell heavenly, my darling."

She could feel the heat rising in her neck and face. "Thank you, Ricardo."

He looked at the window suddenly. "What was that?"

Confused, she listened for the sound he referred to. In the distance, she could hear the thundering of hoof beats. "I think someone's riding up. Who would be calling on us at this time of night?"

He got up, doused the lamp. In the darkness, she could hear the urgency in his voice. "Get down on the floor. Whoever it is, they're coming to make trouble."

CHAPTER FOURTEEN

She obeyed him, but not before reaching into the cushion of her father's chair. Extricating the Colt he had insisted on keeping for protection, she slipped the gun into her wrapper's waist pocket and crouched on the floor.

The sound of hoof beats grew louder, and was soon joined by an unknown number of male voices. Torchlight filled the sitting room as the party drew close to the front porch. In the shadows, she saw Ricardo's hand reach out and grab the Winchester. Readying the weapon, he raised himself slowly, getting a view over the back of the settee.

"There are three mounted men," he whispered. "I want you to stay down. I'll take care of them."

Her whole body trembled. Who knew what horror these men had planned to visit on her household?

Were they cattle rustlers, outlaws, or petty thieves?

Did they have weapons?

His voice interrupted her worrisome thoughts. "Go and hide yourself in the kitchen. And stay down!"

Not knowing what else to do, she followed his instructions. Staying low to the wooden floor, she crawled into the kitchen. Slinking over to the small corner she used as a pantry, she pushed aside a few small barrels of flour, cornmeal, and millet. Sweeping away the dust and cobwebs with her hand, she stifled a sneeze. Then, she pressed herself into the space between the lowest pantry shelf and the floor.

Hunkered in the darkness, she waited.

The front door creaked open, and the footfalls of someone wearing heavy boots could be heard in the silence. Terrified, she covered her mouth to contain her whimpering.

A single gunshot echoed through the house.

A male growl of pain erupted.

But that told her little about who had been on the receiving end of the shot.

Had it been Ricardo, or the stranger?

Worry over Ricardo's well-being overtook her, and a fat tear slid down her cheek. Mindful of his words, she kept silent.

Thump... Something or someone hit the floor.

She could hear them scuffling.

Their muffled grunts and the sounds of furniture being upset overwhelmed her with alarm.

Who had the upper hand?

What would become of Ricardo?

And if he were hurt and unable to protect her, what would she do?

Glass broke, followed by a guttural cry.

Something scraped across the floor.

Struggling for every breath, she did her best to keep calm.

A match was struck, a lamp lit.

Footsteps approached her position. Whoever lit the lamp was carrying it, and she could see the circle of light traveling toward her.

Having no idea whether Ricardo or the stranger held the lamp, she made herself as small as she could, pressing even harder against the wall. Her muscles ached and protested, but she ignored them.

The lantern's glow cast on the kitchen floor.

It was held aloft by a white man of average height and build. She could see his ruddy face, his eyes searching the room.

He stood less than three feet from her.

Too afraid to make a sound, she held her breath.

He swept the lantern, casting the light on her table, her wash tub, her icebox.

He grunted. "Well, we've taken care of the Spaniard. No need to disturb the lady of the house, I suppose."

A crooked smile crossed his face.

He turned, and walked through the living room.

He never looked in her direction.

She kept silent as he moved away from her, but every part of her heart and soul thanked the good Lord in heaven for sparing her.

It was not until she heard the front door close, and the echoing sound of horse's hooves, that she finally drew a gasping breath.

Sputtering and worried out her mind, she extricated herself from her confining hiding spot. She needed more than anything to make sure Ricardo was all right.

She found him, sprawled across the sitting room floor.

Blood pooled around his left side.

She knelt beside his prone, silent form, found the bullet wound in his side. Summoning her strength, she stripped away the blood soaked shirt he wore, buttons flying as she opened it with haste. She winced at the sight of the ugly, red gash. It appeared as if he'd only been grazed, but with only the moonlight to see by, she couldn't be sure.

His left arm also bore a bullet wound, this one much deeper. She assumed the bullet tore through his arm then grazed his side.

The purple bruise on the side of his head, near his hairline, explained his condition. She touched the spot gently with her fingertips.

Lowering her head, she turned to the side, positioning her ear above his nose.

She could hear him taking shallow, labored breaths.

He was alive! Thanks be to God, he had not been killed.

But the wound to his arm was serious. If nothing was done to stop the bleeding, he could be in grave danger.

With no one else around, the task fell to her.

She removed the tablecloth draped over her side table. Folding it into a narrow strip, she wrapped the fabric around his injured arm, and tied it off as tightly as she could manage.

With that done, she stood. She would need to fetch Doc Wilkins, and Sheriff Rogers.

Feeling uncharacteristically sentimental toward her new husband, she gazed at his face. Without hesitation, he had twice put himself at risk to protect her. Even before they were married he'd taken on the responsibility of ensuring her safety. Perhaps he deserved less of her barking and more of her affection.

She lit her lantern, still resting in the windowsill.

Hastily slipping her feet out of her house shoes and into the pair of brogans she kept by the front door, she dashed from the house, lantern in hand. She needed to get a horse from the barn.

The idea of riding the three miles into town at this late hour was less than ideal, but she had no choice.

When she arrived there, she found four of her five stalls unoccupied.

Her face twisted in anger. Those ruffians had stolen her horses!

That made her think. What else had they done?

So, clutching her lantern, she skittered around the area, checking coops and pens. She couldn't account for two of her laying hens, along with a good number of eggs. Her pigs were missing as well. In the darkness, there was no way to tell if the animals had been carted off or simply turned loose on the property. Either way, come daylight she would have her work cut out for her. Locating the livestock, even if they were still on Warren land, would be a chore to say the least.

Irritated beyond her usual capacity, she steeled herself. Someone was going to pay for this, and for hurting Ricardo.

She returned to the barn, opened the stall of the remaining horse. After saddling the brown mare she'd named Empress, she mounted the animal and guided it out of the barn.

Urging Empress to a gallop, she passed the house and rode across the open fields that lay beyond it. The full moon shone above them, illuminating the ground beneath the horse's pounding hooves.

As they approached the grove of pine trees that served as the property line, she could see a shadow of something. It looked like a vehicle of some kind, parked beneath the branches.

"Whoa." She slowed the mare to a trot.

The closer they got, the clearer it became.

It was the same fancy brown carriage she had seen so many times.

Dread filled her, her body tensing atop her mount.

Before the carriage stood the smug, smiling Ezekiel Martindale, his gaze trained on her.

CHAPTER FIFTEEN

Ricardo's eyes snapped open, and the throbbing of his head greeted him.

He was prone on a hard surface. The silver glow of moonlight streamed down on him, cutting through the surrounding darkness.

His left arm burned with a searing pain just below the shoulder.

His left side also pulsated with pain.

Attempting to wriggle his body, he felt a sticky dampness around and beneath him. Inhaling the metallic scent that permeated the air, he recognized the wetness he felt as blood.

He groaned, placing his right hand on his temple. Even lifting his arm to do so proved to be a chore.

He had no idea where he was, or what had happened. His mind was all fog and haze.

He turned his head, lifted it ever so slightly. A crude bandage had been fashioned for him from a piece of cloth. He could see the white fabric, now spotted with his blood, circling his throbbing arm. It was tied so tight he could barely flex his elbow.

How had he gotten injured?

Who attempted to help him?

He struggled to remember...

The haze in his mind swirled, began to change into fuzzy images.

Then the memories revealed themselves.

The mounted men, the fight with their leader.

He'd been shot. The bullet had come from a Colt handgun.

The man had struck him with the butt of the gun and all had gone black.

Lilly!

Where was she?

He recalled telling her to hide in the kitchen.

He listened for any indication of her presence, but heard only the silence and the chirping of crickets outside.

Bracing himself on his right elbow, he tried to sit up. Dizziness attacked him, and he fell back.

Again, he tried to sit up, this time with success. He sat still for few moments, to allow his reeling mind to adjust to the change in positioning. Then, he pushed himself to his knees.

He grasped the edge of the settee with his right hand, and dragged himself to his feet. His balance wobbly at best, he staggered toward the kitchen.

He called out to his wife, praying she would answer. "Lilly, it is me, Bella. Where are you?" Only the silence replied.

A thorough search of the room revealed no sign of Lilly.

Leaning against the door frame, he wondered where she had gone.

Had the men taken her?

If they harmed her, he vowed to personally see them to their graves.

Scanning his surroundings, he noted that the front door of the house stood open.

Gathering his remaining strength, he passed through the room and made his way outside.

On the front porch he paused, opening his ears for some sound that might give him a clue to Lilly's whereabouts.

Over the chirping of crickets, he could hear the barely audible sounds of two voices in the distance.

Somewhere, not too far from where he stood, an argument took place.

One voice was male, and sounded angry.

The other, feminine voice... belonged to his sweet Lilly.

His arm and side still hurt, and his head still throbbed in time with his heartbeat, but it didn't matter. He intended to get to her, to see for himself that she was safe, if it took everything in him.

To that end, he hobbled off the porch and traveled in the direction of the distant sound.

CHAPTER SIXTEEN

Seated in Empress' saddle, Lilly watched Ezekiel warily.

In his right hand he held something shiny and metal. She could see the glint of moonlight reflecting off the object.

"What is the meaning of this?" No matter how nervous she might be, she would not give this fleshy man the satisfaction of knowing it.

He paced the ground, hand behind his back. "I've come to claim what's mine, Lilly."

She groaned inwardly. It would give her great pleasure to shoot the man right where he stood. But if she reached for the weapon now, he would see her. The bright moonlight would give him all the warning he needed to dodge her shots, as well as a man his size could dodge. So she decided to wait for a more opportune moment, because when she shot at him, she wanted to be sure of hitting her target. "Mr. Martindale, as I've told you many times, I have no desire to marry you. Besides, you know I am already married to someone else."

His voice came out in an angry hiss. "That is of no consequence! That sea dog Spaniard is beneath me, and so are you." He inched closer to the horse. "I am a powerful man, Lilly. You will not have a moment's peace until you marry me, and hand over the title to this land."

What a cad! "Did you send those thugs to my home, to steal my animals?"

He laughed bitterly. "I sent them, but to hell with your animals. I gave them orders to get rid of that damn Spaniard!"

Towering above him from her seat on Empress's back, she realized that Ezekiel was more of snake than she'd ever known. How could he do such a thing? Did he really think his money and land claims gave him a right to send a pack of ruffians to trespass on her property? To kill a man, simply because he was a rival for her affections? Well contrary to the fantasy Ezekiel had been entertaining in his own mind, she had no interest in him, therefore, the rivalry didn't even exist.

"Are you really so pigheaded?" She shook her head, and realized she pitied him. "I could never love you. You disgust me, not only with your slovenly, portly appearance, but your attitude that you are somehow better than everyone else."

He pointed a pudgy finger at her, his eyes full of hate. "I may not be better than everyone, but I am sure as hell better than you. Now this is your last chance to marry me and turn over that damn deed!"

Growing tired of his demands, she tugged the reins. "Mr. Martindale, I have had enough of this. I'm riding into town for Sheriff Rogers. Whether you wait here or not, I'm going to see that you are arrested for trespassing on my family's land."

In an instant, Ezekiel's hand swung out, the shiny object revealing itself as a knife. He sliced across the mare's forelegs, and the beast whined in pain.

As the horse toppled down to a kneeling position, Lilly slid off its back and landed on her rear end in the damp grass.

The Colt tumbled out of her pocket, and she quickly sat on it to cover it.

"You brute! You're low enough to injure an animal that way?" She dabbed at the blood dripping from the cuts in Empress's skin with her wrapper, and stroked the horse's mane. The wounds were not very serious, but the animal had been startled.

"That is the least of your concern now, you half-breed tramp," Ezekiel spat. He lunged at her, the knife thrust forward.

He managed to knock her on her back, and she cried out. "Get away from me!"

Leering at her, he knelt over her and slid the blade of the knife near her throat. "You will not keep denying me, I won't have it!"

He reached for the belt of her wrapper, and she slapped his hand aside. "No!"

Reeling back in anger, he struck her across the face. "It is high time you learned your place!" He turned away for a moment to fiddle with the placard of his too tight pants.

That was all the time she needed. Raising her lower body off the ground, she slipped her hand beneath her hips and extricated the Colt. He did not even realize she had it until she clicked the hammer.

Eyes wide with shock and fear, he cowered as she placed the gun in his face.

With coldness and warning in her voice, she instructed, "Move off, Martindale."

He stammered, as if he wanted to speak, but she did not care to hear anything else he had to say.

"I said, move off!" She wanted nothing more than to fill his hide with bullets, but that would land her in jail.

He slid away, his giant behind dragging blades of grass and twigs with it.

"On your feet," she directed him as she stood, the gun still trained on him.

He obeyed, hauling his girth to stand. "Wh...Where are we going?"

"Wherever I say. Now move!" She gestured with the gun in the direction of the house.

When he hesitated, she pressed the gun into his back. That got him moving.

As they went back toward the house, she glanced back at Empress. She vowed to get help for the horse as soon as she could, but right now she had pressing business to attend to.

They made it only a few yards before she saw a figure approaching.

CHAPTER SEVENTEEN

Ricardo staggered into the clearing that led to the tree line of the property, and to his surprise, he saw Ezekiel Martindale. The large man held both his hands up in surrender as he approached his position.

At first, confusion gripped Ricardo.

Then he saw Lilly. She was walking behind him, and had something pressed into the large man's back.

He closed the distance quickly. "Lilly, are you all right, my darling?" He saw the gun she used to subdue

Martindale and smiled.

But as he looked at her more closely, saw the blood on the front of her wrapper, the smile disappeared from his face.

He didn't give her a chance to answer his question.

In a heartbeat, he pounced on Ezekiel.

The larger man grunted, falling to the ground.

Ricardo stayed on top of him, pounding his right fist into Ezekiel's face. Driven by rage, he ignored the searing pain coursing through his body.

This sack of lard had hurt his sweet Lilly, and he was going to pay for his crime with a pound of flesh.

In the fog of anger that surrounded and spurred him, he heard her voice calling his name. Suspending his assault on the now bloodied Ezekiel, he looked up.

"Ricardo, what are you doing? I have never seen you act so brutish."

He gestured to the streaked blood on her wrapper. "There is blood on you. He has harmed you."

She shook her head. "He has harmed Empress, my mare. This is her blood."

"Oh." Feeling somewhat presumptuous, but not regretting putting the rude, arrogant man in his place, he released his grip and dropped him to the ground.

Ezekiel lay in a heap in the damp grass, coughing, sputtering, and cursing.

Ignoring him, Ricardo wiped the sweat from his brow with the back of his hand, and stood. Grasping her hands, he spoke. "I vowed to protect you, and this land," he insisted, gritting his teeth against the searing pain in his body.

She smiled, and his heart sang. "Considering the fact that you are injured, and you still did this for me, I must admit I am impressed."

"Good. Then I have a chance at winning you yet, my darling."

He could see her honey brown cheeks filling with red under the moonlight. "We need to get to town. You need to see Doc Wilkins, and we shall leave Mr. Martindale in the custody of Sheriff Rogers."

He nodded. "Agreed. I will need something for this nagging pain."

"Get up, Martindale," she demanded of the prone man, pointing the Colt at him.

Ricardo helped her drag the grumbling land baron to his feet, and they set off toward his waiting carriage. Once they arrived, Lilly drove the four horse team, and Ricardo sat in the back with Martindale, the Colt trained on him for the duration of the three mile ride to town.

Once in town, they parked Martindale's fancy carriage in front of the building that held the sheriff's office, mayor's office, and jail. When they entered, they found Deputy Sheriff Gregory Simmons working the late shift. His face registered shock as Ricardo and Lilly hauled the bloodied, furious Martindale into the place.

"Evenin', Miss Lilly, Captain Benigno. What is this all about?" The lawman sat up at his desk.

Lilly spoke. "Mr. Martindale was trespassing on my property, injured my horse, and threatened me."

Deputy Simmons nodded, then turned to Ricardo. "Am I to assume that is why he is looking so beat up?"

"Yes." Ricardo gestured to Martindale. "And I am sure you would love to hear about the band of thugs he sent to the house ahead of him."

The deputy frowned. "Well, Mr. Martindale, looks like you'll be staying with me. Me and Sheriff Rogers have know Lilly since she was a babe. She's an honest woman, and we won't have her terrorized."

Ezekiel sputtered. "You are not going to take the word of the likes of them, are you?"

Ricardo sighed. The man simply could not deal with being put in his place.

"I sure am." The deputy stood, and unceremoniously tossed the angry faced, cursing man into one of the two vacant cells.

"Thank you," she offered. Turning to Ricardo, she added, "Now, we are getting you over to Doc Wilkins."

They left the jail, and the furious, ranting Ezekiel Martindale behind.

CHAPTER EIGHTEEN

Ricardo reclined in bed, flexing his arm. Since Doc Wilkins had patched him up in the wee hours of the morning, Lilly had prohibited him from doing anything, banishing him to the bedroom to rest. The doctor had decreed that with proper rest and wound care, he'd be back to normal within a fortnight. With both his side and his arm freshly bandaged, and a dose of willow bark tea dulling his pain, he felt well enough to sit up.

What he really wanted was to be outside with Lilly, helping her search for the missing livestock. While he understood the importance of following the doctor's orders to speed his healing, he was bored to tears. He was used to spending his days at sea, going over reports, tallying inventories, and checking weather conditions with his spyglass. In the five days since he'd come home to Lilly, things had been very different.

Home. That perfectly described how he felt with her in his arms. In such a short time, his beautiful, feisty wife had worked her way into his heart and soul. He knew life with her would require much compromise, but would also gift him with a happiness beyond anything he ever expected to experience.

The mid afternoon heat that had become trapped in the house was broken by a cool breeze flowing through the open shutters. He swung his legs over the side of the bed, intent on getting to the desk to retrieve the copy of the Ridgeway Gazette she left there.

As he dragged himself across the room, he heard her clear her throat. "And just where do you think you're going, Captain?"

Again she referred to him so formally? "For Poseidon's sake, woman, call me Ricardo."

She shook her head, smiling as she approached to help him back to bed. "Not until you start following Doc Wilkins' orders to rest."

Easing back into the bed, he sighed. "I have been very good. I only wanted the newspaper."

Fetching the newspaper from the top of her desk, she handed it to him.

"What became of the animals?" He waited for her answer.

"I located most of them on the property." Lilly pulled a bit of bramble from her hair. "We are still short one hen, a piglet, and two horses, but I suppose that can not be helped. They will likely wander back here eventually, if they were not stolen."

"I would suggest you take the remainder of the day off. You look as though you had quite a morning adventure." She was covered in grime, from her dirt streaked face to the leaves and pine burrs clinging to her clothing.

The smile she gave him appeared sincere. He couldn't be sure, but he thought he saw admiration in her gaze.

"Have I thanked you for acting so gallantly on my behalf?"

He nodded. "Yes, but I never tire of hearing it, my darling."

She stroked his cheek. "If you had not ordered me to hide, and fought off those thugs, who knows what would have become of me?" She looked into his eyes, her own gaze filled with emotion. "I can never repay you."

Her admission touched his heart. "I was merely doing my duty as your husband, Lilly." He clasped her hand, pressed it to his lips. "And I would do it again. Besides, the bandage you placed on my arm may well have saved my life."

She looked away, blushing. "My little makeshift bandage? I do not think that measures up to you beating the tar out of Ezekiel Martindale, simply because you suspected he hurt me."

Ricardo wasn't a man prone to violence, but he had thoroughly enjoyed doling out the beating Martindale so richly deserved. "You might be right about that," he stated jokingly, "but I appreciate your efforts nonetheless."

"I realize I have not been the most agreeable wife." She cringed, looking as if she regretted her previous words and actions. "I apologize for my behavior. Pa would be appalled, as I am."

He felt genuine appreciate fill him as she humbled herself to him. She'd been hurt by having those soiled doves brought onto her property, he was well aware of that. But at least now she seemed willing to forgive his lapse in judgment, and he was glad to hear it. "I understand. We are still getting to know one another." Still clutching her hand, he pulled her atop his lap. "All is forgiven, as long as you agree to call me Ricardo again."

She leaned against his chest, sighing with contentment. "I suppose I can agree to that."

His deep voice just above a whisper, he confessed, "You may be headstrong, but you are beautiful, and passionate, and in a few short days, I have grown to love you."

She jumped. With wide eyes, she met his gaze. "What?"

"I said, I love you, Lilly."

She sucked in a breath. "Well, that is a relief, because I love you, too, Ricardo. So much so that I long to bear your children. I love you," she repeated.

Delighted, he gave her a wide grin. "Truly, my darling?"

She kissed his forehead. "Truly."

Relief washed over him. Now that they had shared their feelings, perhaps things would become easier and less awkward between them.

"You know," she purred, stroking his face, "I would love to take a sea voyage for our honeymoon."

He stiffened, turned away from her caress. He made great effort to afford her gaze.

Her expression confused, she asked, "What is the matter?"

"I do not wish to go back to sea," he replied in a monotonous, gruff tone.

"Why?"

Struggling to maintain a calm demeanor despite his annoyance, Ricardo groaned. He had vowed never to let Lilly discover his weakness. But from the questioning look she wore, he could tell she would persist until he answered her.

"Well, Ricardo," she pressed, arms folded across her chest, "why can we not enjoy a wedding cruise?"

In his condition, rising from the bed and leaving the room seemed ill advised. His injuries would slow him down, and she would follow him, continuing to fire off questions like balls from a cannon. He closed his eyes, released a pent up breath. "Lilly, I can not get back on a ship."

"You already said that. What you have not told me is why."

He sighed. What would she think of him, now that she was forcing the truth out of him. "I contracted an incurable case of vertigo several months ago, and I am unable to tolerate the reeling and rocking of the vessel." He slid his bottom on the bed's surface, turned toward the window so he did not have to face her and reveal the shame on his face. "There, I have told you. Are you satisfied?

She was silent for a moment. "Is that why you came here? Because you could not remain on your ship due to something over which you have no control?" Her voice sounded soft, sympathetic.

"I genuinely wanted to visit Leonard, but yes." He balled his hands into fists. "I could no longer remain aboard the Anna Juanita. Every time she hit a wave, my balance abandoned me." He could still hear the laughter and taunting of his crew, and he pushed away the memories, along with the anger and frustration that accompanied them.

Her hand stroked his bare back, and whether she knew it or not, her touch presented its very own brand of comfort. "Ricardo, why did you not tell me this before?"

He almost chuckled at the question, but held himself in check. How could she have expected him to be honest with her, when her manner toward him had been so abrasive? Grasping his composure, her turned back to face her. "I didn't want you to know my weakness, darling. You should be confident in my ability to protect and provide for you."

A sweet, gentle smile lit her lovely face. "And I am no less confident in you than I was last night, when you were beating the grit out of Ezekiel."

That made him return her smile. "I would appreciate it if this remained between us, Lilly."

She nodded, kissed his cheek softly. Her eyes held the promise of her loyalty, and she seemed content to press him no further. For that, he felt grateful.

A pounding sound from downstairs interrupted them.

"Someone is at the door," she announced, standing and smoothing her rumpled skirt. "I will see who has come to call on us." With a wave, she left the room.

CHAPTER NINETEEN

Padding down the steps in her slipper covered feet, Lilly went to the door and opened it. On the other side stood a bald Hispanic man, whose face she vaguely remembered. "Yes, can I help you?"

"Hello, Señora Benigno. I'm sorry to disturb you, but I need to see Ricardo, it is urgent."

His words tumbled out so fast she almost missed that he called her by her married name. Feeling the heat rise to her cheeks, she composed herself. "Ricardo is injured... we had some trespassers on the property last night, and he was shot in the melee. Would you like to visit with him, Mr..." She waited for him to volunteer his name.

His water green eyes widened. He seemed very distressed as he shouted, "Ricardo has been hurt?" Seeing her reaction to his raised voice, he looked apologetic. "Oh, forgive me, Señora. I am Antonio, the new captain of the Anna Juanita." He bowed.

She stepped aside to allow him entrance. As she turned to go upstairs, she saw Ricardo hobbling down on his own. He gripped the banister with his right hand and took slow, deliberate steps.

"Antonio, what are you doing here?" Ricardo turned questioning eyes on his friend. "I could hear you upstairs."

He moved to aid his old friend, concern lining his face. "Ricardo, what has happened to you?"

Ricardo gave a brief explanation of the visit from Martindale and his thugs, with Lilly filling in the parts Ricardo had missed.

When the tale was told, an angry expression replaced the worry on Antonio's face. "Where is this

Martindale and his ruffians? The crew will see to their punishment."

As Lilly looked on in amazement, Ricardo waved him off with his good arm. "No need. The sheriff will take care of it. "

Still looking angry, Antonio acquiesced. "All right, if that's what you wish. I would still enjoy the chance to maroon them, though."

"Maroon?" Lilly had no idea what he was speaking of.

"That means leaving a person on an uninhabited island, with a loaded pistol and several days worth of food," her husband explained.

She shivered at the suggestion. While she disliked Martindale greatly, she thought jail punishment enough for him. She realized she might have welcomed the idea had Ricardo been killed.

"Also, I'd like to apologize to you, Senora." Antonio bowed in her direction. "Ricardo gave me quite the lecture for bringing those whores here, and I regret disrespecting you."

Touched by his apology, and the sincerity she sensed, she nodded. "Thank you, Captain."

Ricardo cleared his throat. "I'm growing quite sore, amigo. Why is it you have come here?"

"I'd like you to return to the vessel, but I understand if you do not wish to come."

He looked surprised, then shook his head. "No. I am no longer the captain of the vessel. That responsibility is now yours."

Antonio placed a hand on his shoulder. "Please come. It is Victoria."

Lilly raised a brow, folded her arms across her chest. "And just who might this Victoria be?"

Ricardo glanced at her with an annoyed look, then turned a blank stare on Antonio. "I do not know a Victoria."

"Ah, but you do. She is the fair haired prostitute who attended your frolic."

Lilly clasped a hand to her forehead in disbelief. Apparently, this loose woman thought showing up at her wedding, bawling like someone in mourning, was insufficient rudeness.

"Well, what of her? I can not imagine what she could be doing on the ship, and why you would seek me out?" Ricardo propped his hands on his hips, watching his friend with expectation.

"She crept onto the ship." Antonio pulled him toward the door. "Then she shimmied up the center mast with a Derringer, and threatened to do herself harm." He drew a deep breath, recovering the air he expelled making his speech. "She demands to speak to you."

"*Dios mio*," Ricardo whispered. Turning to Lilly with a pitiful expression, he launched into an apology. "Lilly, I had no idea she would..."

She raised a hand, stopping him in mid-sentence. "Ricardo, we do not have time for this. If you recall, I have plenty of experience with having a loon set their cap for me, as well." Sliding her feet out of her slippers and into her brogans, she righted herself and faced him. "We need to go to the ship and see about the girl before she hurts herself, or someone else."

"I came on horseback," Antonio volunteered. "It was the fastest way to get here."

"Well, he can not sit a horse, nor drive a team with his arm bandaged," she said, gesturing toward the door. "So I will drive him to the harbor."

Ricardo looked put out, as if he did not care for her take charge attitude, but said nothing. She supposed he wanted to avoid having his friend see them at odds.

Antonio nodded his understanding, and the three of them walked out into the front yard. Once Ricardo was on the seat of her buggy, Antonio mounted his horse and urged the beast to a trot. Soon she was behind the reins of her two horse team, and she drove them in the direction Antonio traveled.

CHAPTER TWENTY

Arriving at the harbor, Ricardo wanted dearly to leap out of the buggy and see what was really happening aboard the vessel. When the buggy came to a halt, his attempt to turn his body in preparation for the jump to the ground caused pain to radiate through his left side. He drew a sharp breath, grimaced.

Lilly shook her head. "Ricardo, I will help you down. Do not overexert yourself." She got down on her side.

Gritting his teeth, he slid to the ground, steadying himself against the buggy's side. "See, I am perfectly capable of doing it myself."

"If you insist."

Looking ahead, he could see Antonio, already rushing up the gangplank. He waited patiently for him to join him, and he silently thanked his friend for taking his injuries into consideration.

With Lilly grasping his good arm, Ricardo made his way up the plank and onto the three masted barque his brother had dubbed the Anna Juanita. Even as he stepped aboard, he could hear female sobbing. He could not recall the last time the crew had been so silent. They all stood, as if bonded to their posts, staring up.

Antonio stood among them on the main deck, pointing skyward. Shifting his gaze upward, Ricardo saw the fair haired Victoria, clinging to the center mast, about halfway up its height. Her garish blue dress and blond locks billowed in the breeze flowing over the water, her painted face distorted and running from her tears.

Beneath him, the vessel swayed slightly from the motion of the water beneath it. He tipped forward a bit.

He heard Lilly gasp, felt her clutch his right arm tightly.

The sun illuminated the shimmering pearl handle of the small gun stuck in Victoria's ample bosom.

Victoria, seeming to notice him for the first time, composed herself. "Hello, Captain," she cooed from her perch.

"Hello, Victoria." He chose his words carefully. "What brings you to the Anna Juanita?"

"A voyage, Captain. I am going to take a sea voyage." A false brightness filled her voice. "I wish to see the shore of another land before I take my life."

She let loose one hand's grip on the mast, dangling precariously over the deck.

He held his breath.

Finally she clutched the mast with both hands again.

He could feel the sweat gathering on his brow. Victoria appeared irrational, as if under the influence of a large quantity of alcohol. He had never encountered such a situation before, but felt he should try to dissuade her from causing herself harm. "Victoria, taking your life is not a good idea."

She laughed bitterly. "And why not? Have you come to denounce your marriage, declare your affections for me?"

As unstable as she looked, Ricardo considered lying to her. With the water churning and the boat rocking, he did his best to hold his balance. His wife's support did much to steady him.

Victoria spoke again before he had a chance. "Do not pretend, Captain. What would a man like you want with a used up soiled dove like me? If I ended it right now," she declared, pulling the Derringer from her cleavage, "no one would mourn my passing." She waved the gun about before placing the barrel to her heart.

His mind reeled as he tried to formulate a suitable response, the process complicated by the loss of his balance. Obviously life had dealt her an unfriendly hand, but he had no idea how to convince her life remained worthwhile.

Lilly spoke up. "I would mourn you."

Gripped by surprise, he stared at his wife, who still clutched his arm. Then he looked back to Victoria.

Victoria's sorrowful expression had changed to one of confusion, and some other emotion he could not determine. In a wavering voice, Victoria asked, "Why would you mourn a whore?"

"Because," Lilly called, surety in every word, "My Pa taught me that every human life is valuable, no matter the circumstances." She let go of his arm, walked closer to the mast. At its base, she stopped and gazed up. "And I believe that to be true."

He took two shaky steps backward, and leaned on the ship's sidewall to maintain his standing position as he watched the scene play out.

Victoria's eyes grew wide, and he could almost sense a calm washing over the distraught woman. Opening her hand, she let the gun slip from her grasp. It clattered to the wooden deck below, and one of the crew men picked it up.

In a soft, throaty voice, she called, "If a good woman like you can lower yourself to care about me, then I suppose I will come down."

Lilly nodded. "Good, but I don't consider you lower than I." She turned to the men speckling the deck. "Gentlemen, please assist Victoria from the mast."

Ricardo could do nothing more than stare as she returned to his side. While efforts were made to retrieve Victoria, he stood there, looking into his wife's eyes, filled with amazement. With her caring heart and calm head, she had saved a human life. Even though she looked completely unaffected by her deed, in his eyes, her status had been elevated tremendously. He had thought it impossible to love her more, but she had succeeded in proving him wrong.

"Why do you regard me so?" she asked.

It was the same question she had asked him the night of his arrival. So much had happened since then, but his answer remained largely the same. "I am simply admiring your beauty... only now, I see it comes from within."

She smiled and looked down at the deck floor beneath her. Redness filled her cheeks.

"You have saved a human life. I think this is cause for celebration." His gaze grew heated and his eyes took on a wicked gleam.

"Oh, and just what sort of celebration do you have in mind?" She stroked her hand along the sinewy hardness of his bare chest.

"Allow me to show you." He clasped her hand. After saying their goodbyes, and receiving assurances from Antonio that Victoria would be well cared for, they departed.

Along the deserted road back to their farm, he directed her to pull the buggy over into a clearing at the edge of a pine forest.

"Why are we stopping here?"

He reached out, stroked her face with his right hand. "I must show you my affections, Lilly, and I can not wait until we make it home." With heated stroking and equally torrid kisses, he coaxed her out of her shirtwaist and onto his lap atop the buggy's seat.

***

And show Lilly he did, with amorous abandon. The evening breeze washed over Lilly's bare skin, cooling all the places left damp by his kiss. Only the songs of insects and birds competed with the beautiful melody of their own creation. When the sun began to set, painting the sky with a tableau of rich colors, she sang his name on the wings of release.

He kissed her dampened brow. "Oh, Lilly, how I love you," he whispered against the shell of her ear.

"And I you, Ricardo." More than she had ever imagined possible to love a man. As apprehensive as she had initially been, she now loved this dashing Spaniard as she loved breathing.

In the evening stillness, she sighed with contentment. And as she lay there, her body entwined with his, she knew that she would be blessed to spend the rest of her days kissing her captain.

EPILOGUE

Spring's blush faded into the sweltering heat of summer. Being accustomed to the sea breezes in Barcelona, Ricardo welcomed the cooler autumn months like a long lost friend. Sitting on the front porch of the farmhouse in one of the old rockers, he sipped from a tumbler of Lilly's tart lemonade. The warm afternoon sun shone in rays through the poplar trees.

Hoof beats and the creaking of their wagon wheels heralded Lilly's approach. She'd gone into town earlier that day to retrieve the post and pick up some items from the mercantile.

As she parked the vehicle and set the hand brake, he stepped off the porch to assist her down. Once she was on the ground, she melted into his welcoming embrace, and he planted a long kiss on her full, ripe lips. "How was your morning, my love?"

She smiled, wiping a hand across her brow. "Quite full, I'm afraid. I'm very tired." Reaching into the front pocket of her brown skirt, she extricated an envelope. "This was at the post office for you."

Taking the letter from her outstretched hand, he looked at the postmark. His eyes widened with surprise, and he felt a wide grin spreading across his face. "It's a letter from my father."

She looked interested. "By all means, let's read it. We'll take the flour and millet in a little later."

They climbed the four steps and took their seats on the rockers next to each other and the upturned barrel table between them. With quick fingers, he tore open the envelope, and extricated the paper inside. Seeing his father's handwriting after all these months away from home nearly brought a tear to his eye. Clearing his throat, he read aloud.

Dear Son,

I have received correspondence from a Maxwell Peters, who tells me you have inherited a large parcel of land from my old shipping amigo, Leonard Warren. I also understand that you have inherited his daughter as a bride. I remember Lilly as a young girl. If she has grown into the lovely, intelligent woman I imagine, then you have acquired a great treasure. I offer my congratulations to you, Ricardo. I only hope your brother Hernando will one day settle down with a woman of proper upbringing. Your mother sends her love and good wishes as well, and wishes to know when you will give her little nietos to spoil. Please write when you can. Live well, my son.

Your Father,

Diego Benigno

Ricardo refolded the paper and tucked it back into the envelope. Turning his eyes to Lilly, he found her brushing away a tear.

"What is it, Bella?"

"I had no idea your father thought so highly of me." A blush of redness filled her tawny cheeks.

Her modesty brought a smile to his lips. "I think highly of you as well, Lilly."

She reached out and stroked her satin fingertips along the edge of his newly grown beard. "I'm glad. Because we are about to grant your mother's wish."

Confusion filled him. "What do you mean?"

With a sparkle in those liquid dark eyes, she came to sit on his lap. In the circle of his arms, she placed both his hands on her belly. "We are having a baby, Ricardo."

He wanted to leap for joy, but thought the better of it to avoid jostling his delicate wife, and the life she sheltered in her womb. "How do you know this?'

"One of the stops I made today was to Doc Wilkins' office." A sly look graced her face. "I suspected this, but I wanted to be sure before I told you."

Joy filled his heart. He had never before experienced such a feeling of bliss as he did in that moment, holding the love of his life. Wonder and love coursed through him as he thought of the babe, growing inside her, beneath the very spot where his hands lay. "Lilly, I love you, ma bella."

"I love you, too," she whispered, her head falling against his chest.

He let his chin rest in the top of her silky hair, and held her close. No amount of money, fame, or time spent at sea compared to this.

This was bliss.

And he couldn't be more grateful.

The End

A NOTE FROM THE AUTHOR

-Explore love, life, and the challenges of a bygone era.-

<u>Ridgeway, California:</u>

A mixed race settlement founded by abolitionists in 1853, after the California gold rush died down.

<u>The Roses of Ridgeway</u>:

The feisty, determined female citizens of the settlement.

-Look out for the next story, <u>The Preachers' Paramour</u>, coming summer 2012.-

Prudence Emerson doesn't have time for romantic entanglements. She's taken a job at the mercantile, and is saving money to attend school at Oberlin. That is, until the Reverend Derrick Chase rides into town to start a new church. She can't deny her attraction to him, and the handsome mulatto preacher obviously returns the feelings. Should she change her plans to explore a relationship with him? Or will being the preacher's paramour lead to nothing but pain?

Made in the USA
Lexington, KY
14 June 2014